The Heart's Country

Mary Heaton Vorse

CONTENTS

PROLOGUE

The actors in this drama are dead, or else life has turned them into such different beings that their transformation is hardly less than that of death itself. Their thoughts are scattered to the winds, or live, oddly changed, in the bodies of their children—the girl who brought me the journals and packages of letters smiled up at me with the flashing smile of Ellen.

This girl, with a gesture of the hand, opened for me the gates of the past, and when she was gone I walked through them with beating heart, back over the steep path of years. This little package of long-forgotten papers which she had given me, and of whose contents she was ignorant, were a strange legacy, for it was my own youth that I found in them and the youth of Ellen.

As I went over the scrawled journals and through the packages of letters, the land of memory blossomed for me and the tears that came to my eyes thawed the ice of many years. Ellen herself had forgotten her youth; she may not have remembered that in the bottom of an old trunk she had left for me things which she could not bear to destroy—for there they found them after her death with a letter addressed to me. As I read on, it was as though I had before me the broken pieces of her heart, and as I looked, my own childhood and even my girlhood lived again.

I had often looked for my girlhood and had never found it. Those years when women are in the making—that land of glamour—are the hardest thing of all for grown-up people to understand. Nothing stays fixed there, all the emotions are at their point of effervescence and their charm is their evanescence. The very power of early youth is in the violence of its changes; it is the era of chaos in the souls of people; when they are in the making; when the crust is only forming, and the fire may break forth at any moment; and when what seems most secure and fixed trembles under the feet and disappears in some new-made gulf of the emotions. Then, too, in our youth they teach us such cruel things, we spend ourselves in trying to keep alive such spent fires, and no one tells us that it is anything but noble to live under the destructive tyranny of love. We have to find our way alone—

The thought came to me that I would try to write a sort of story of my friend. And yet, although I had before me the picture of a heart in the making, I have taken up my pen and laid it down again because it is not a story which "marches." Its victories and defeats went on in the quiet of Ellen's heart, but I have learned that this silent making and marring of the hearts of women means the fate of all men forever.

I fancy that women will have another bar of judgment and that the question asked us there will be: "Have you loved well? Were you small and grudging and niggardly? Did you make of love a sorry barter, or did you give with such a gesture as spring makes when it walks blossoming across the land?" I do not think that old age often repents the generosities of its youth; perhaps it is my own too careful sowing that makes me wish to write the life of my friend, who asked only to spend herself and her own sweetness with both reckless hands.

CHAPTER I

Ellen and her mother drove in a "shay" to take possession of the old Scudder house, which had been vacant long enough to have a deserted and haunted look. It was far back from the street and was sentineled on either side by an uncompromising fir tree. Great vans, of the kind used in that early day to move furniture from one town to another, disgorged their contents on the young spring grass, and though Mildred Dilloway and Janie Acres and I walked to the village store and back on a half-dozen errands, we saw nothing of the new little girl that day; but there remains in my mind the memory of her little mother, a youthful, black-clad figure, moving helplessly, and it seemed at random, among her household effects that squatted so forlornly in the front yard and then started on their processional walk to the house, impelled by the puissant force of Miss Sarah Grant.

Ellen's account of this time is as follows:—

"We are going to live by ourselves, though we can't afford it, because we are ourselves, mamma says, and will really give less trouble this way, though my aunt and uncle think not. 'I want you to win your aunt and uncle,' she said to me. It will be so much easier for me to win them if they don't know me too well. That is one of her reasons for not living in the house with them. 'They would find us so slack that we should become a thorn in their flesh.' 'Couldn't we stop being slack?' I said. Mamma looked at me, and after a long time she said, 'You and I, Ellen, will always be slack inside. Material things don't interest us.' My mother doesn't know me. I like some material things, like ploughing. I said to her: 'Wouldn't they be a thorn in our flesh?' She tried not to smile, and said quite sternly: 'Ellen, you must never think of your dear aunt and uncle in that way.' If it is so, why shouldn't I think so, I wonder? As soon as I saw them I knew what mother meant. They are very nice and I love them, but they have never leaned over the gate to talk to peddlers. A lost dog wouldn't be happy in their home. We have never had any dogs but lost ones. And Aunt Sarah didn't like Faro's name or his ways. I like Aunt Sarah. She says just what she feels like saying. Mother doesn't. Mother says the things she wants to feel like saying. I annoyed my Aunt Sarah by forgetting to come home to help, and mother said, 'Oh, dear, why did you need to go and read the Bible to that woman next door when we were moving in, and I wanted your aunt to have a high opinion of you?' I said, 'She had the rheumatism.' Aunt Sarah said, 'Does she read with her knee; and how came you there anyway, Ellen?' I said, 'By the back door, because I like back doors and I hate going in front doors.' Aunt Sarah looked at me very sharply and said, 'That child of yours, Emily, is just such a child as I should expect you to have, reading the Bible to strangers who have the rheumatism when a pair of willing hands would have been useful at home.' The way she looked at me, I knew deep inside she didn't really mind, so I suddenly kissed her. Later mother said, 'Mercy! I would never have dared to kiss your Aunt Sarah like that.' I told her I knew Aunt Sarah wanted me to. 'How can you tell?' asked mother; but I always know things like that. It makes me feel rather vain, and vanity is a sin. My Uncle Ephraim is like a picture and so is the big house they live in. I had a moment that mamma called 'flesh-pottish' and longed to live there. 'That's just it, Ellen,' she said. 'They are like pictures, and you and I would be sure to injure their lovely surfaces. We are not violent, but so careless.'"

After this arduous day I remember Miss Sarah popped down in my grandmother's sitting-room. Said she: "I'm all out of breath." My grandmother waited for further information. "I've been settling," Miss Sarah informed her with that frankness that kept all the older ladies in town in a state of twittering expectation. "I've been settling my do-less sister and her do-less child." She spoke in some exasperation.

My grandmother allowed a long pause and said reflectively:—

"You'd make any one do-less, Sarah."

And, indeed, Miss Sarah Grant was one of those energetic ladies who leave no place for the energies of others to expand. But here the wind shifted and her irritation disappeared.

"Oh, my dear," she said, "it's too sad. Those children are as little fit to take care of themselves and to live alone as young robins in the nest."

"The Lord looks after such," said my grandmother.

"Well," replied Miss Sarah, with asperity, "you may be sure that after what I've seen of this world I'm not going to leave it with the Lord." She was on terms of familiarity with the Deity that even permitted criticism of his ways. Then she said: "Send Roberta soon to see that poor, fatherless Ellen of mine."

This my grandmother did, shortly afterwards, and I started forth on my first visit to the "poor, fatherless Ellen" at the slow and elegant gait of a hearse with plumes. We were not far removed from that period when young ladies employed their leisure by limning lachrymose females weeping over urns. We were therefore expectant of a certain pomp of mourning; long, black draperies were the least we demanded. Ellen, I learned, was in the apple orchard, and thither I bent my solemn footsteps.

It was in full bloom, one tree after another looking like bridal nosegays of some beneficent giant. All was quiet save for the droning of honey-bees. Suddenly two inches above my head there burst forth the roars of an infant of tender years. I looked up and there I beheld my tragic heroine. Her dress was of blue, checked gingham, a piece of which was caught on a twig of the apple tree and rent nearly in a three-cornered tear. One stocking was coming down in a manner unbecoming to any girl. Her hair was plaited in two neat little "plats," as we used to call them, and tied tightly with meager ribbons; but though I took these things in at a glance, that which naturally most arrested my attention was the fact that Ellen cherished to her bosom a large, red-headed infant, whom I immediately recognized as being one of the brood of the prolific Sweeneys.

The child ceased roaring for a moment, upon which Ellen remarked to me with grave self-composure:—

"How do you do? I suppose you have come to play with me, but my brother and I can't come down for a moment until I have managed to get my dress from that twig. Perhaps you could come up and undo it, or if you could perhaps come and get him—"

"Your brother!" I cried. "That's one of the Sweeney children."

Ellen's eyes flashed. "It is my brother," she insisted. "You can see for yourself it's my brother. Would one have taken anything but one's brother up a tree? I have to take care of him all the time."

Said I: "I've known the Sweeney boys all my life; there are seven of them and the third but one biggest always takes care of the smallest. There's one littler 'n this."

"Oh, there is!" said Ellen. Her brow darkened. "And I got up the tree with this large, hulking thing in my arms—and goodness knows how I ever did get up it!" She spoke with vigor and precision.

"Aha!" I cried, "you say yourself it's a Sweeney."

"I say nothing of the kind," rejoined Ellen. "This is my brother. Come," she wheedled, "why won't you say it's my brother?"

I bit my lip; I wanted to go, for I was not used to being made game of. Moreover, I disapproved of her present position extremely. There was I, my mouth made up, so to speak, for a weeping-willow air, lachrymose ringlets, dark-rimmed eyes, and black raiment, and I had encountered fallen stockings, torn blue gingham, and the Sweeney baby, and the whole of it together up a tree.

Ellen now looked down on me. Her generous mouth with its tip-tilted corners—an exotic, lovable mouth, too large for beauty, but of a remarkable texture and color—now drooped and her eyes filled,—filled beautifully, and yet did not brim over. And for all the droop of the mouth, the saddest little smile I have ever seen hovered about its corners.

"Won't you please say that this is my brother?" she pleaded.

Though I knew it was the Sweeney baby and though I knew she was play-acting all of it, stubborn and downright child though I was, something gripped my heart. Though I couldn't have then put it into words, there was a wistfulness and a heart-hunger about her that played a game with me. It was my first encounter and my first overthrow.

"Have it your brother," said I in a surly fashion.

When we had got the baby down from the tree, Ellen finished me by looking at me with her sincere, sweet eyes in which there was a hint of tears, and saying softly: "Once I had a little brother who died." That was all. She turned her face away; I turned my face away; our hands met. It was as though she was explaining to me her insistence on the Sweeney baby.

It was her look and this silent and averted hand-clasp that brought me to my feet in a very torrent of feeling when Alec Yorke, an engaging youth of eleven summers, came ramping through the orchard shouting:—

"Oh, you'll get it! You'll get it! Mrs. Sweeney's given Ted a good one already—she's after you!"

It was not the gusto in his tone at her ultimate fate that irritated me, but this taking away of Ellen's baby brother.

"Mrs. Sweeney's got nothing to do with this baby!" I cried. "It's Ellen's brother!"

I bent down and picked up a stone and threw it at Alec. Ellen did the same. In one second we had performed one of those amazing sleights of hand that are so frequent and so disconcerting at this moment of girlhood. A moment before we had been swimming along the upper levels of sentiment and crossing the tender, heart-breaking line of the love of women for little children; now our teary mistiness vanished and we were back at the green-apple-hearted moment of childhood. That afternoon I had already been a young lady with all the decorous manners of eighteen; I had been no age,—just a woman whose heart is touched with pity and affection; and now I was just stern, hard twelve, and I threw a rock at my little friend, Alec Yorke. So did Ellen.

Together, with hoots and pebbles, we drove the invading male from our midst. Ellen, I remember, had a "Yip! Yip! Yip!" which was blood-thirsty and derisive at once. She barked it out like a terrier gone mad. I remember also her crying out in a ferocious agony of desire: "Oh, if I get near you, won't I spit on you!"

These were her first words to Alec. He said in later years that their first meeting was indelibly engraven on his memory. He retreated over the fence vanquished by superior force, but with his head well up and his thumb to his gallantly tilted nose. Here Ellen turned to me, the light of victory flashing from her eyes, which fought with my interrogatory gaze, filled with tears again, and at last sought the distance.

"I never had a little brother," she muttered thickly.

Anger surged over me and then died as quickly as it had come. Again she had me. The quiver in her voice showed me what her sincerity had cost her, and so did her next words:—

"I wanted one so always that I just had to make-believe."

Here one had the heart of truth, stripped of the spirit of make-believe which it had clothed in quaint and absurd garments. Again I squeezed Ellen's hand in mine.

I tell all these things in detail because this was so Ellen. She had this dual nature which fought forever in her heart,—the passion for make-believe and the fundamental need of telling the truth,— always to herself, and often embarrassingly to those she loved.

She comments as follows on this episode, unconsciously showing me as the young prig I was:—

"The moment Roberta picked up a rock to fight for my brother, I knew I should have to tell her the truth. I saw right away how good Roberta was. She has very lovely blue eyes and her hair is so smooth and shiny that I don't believe she musses it when she sleeps. She looked at me so straight and her eyes were so round that it was very hard work to tell her that the Sweeney baby was not my brother, but I gritted my teeth and did it. The rest was easy on account of her soft heart."

CHAPTER II

The heart of man is mysterious. Why a passionately expressed desire to spit upon one should be alluring, God knows—I don't. It was fatal to Alec. I see him now jumping up and down outside the fence, shouting forth: "Ya ha! Ya ha! You can't get me!"—or wooing Ellen by the subtle method of attaching a hard green apple to a supple stick and flinging it at her. The relations of these two, as you can see, were deep from the first.

Ellen, more than any of the rest of us, had sharp recrudescences back to little girlhood just as she flamed further ahead on the shimmering path of adolescence. Thus she covered a wide gamut of years in her everyday life. I think it is this ability to roam up and down time that makes life interesting, more than any other thing.

So when Janie Acres and Mildred Dilloway and Ellen and I would be sitting under the trees discussing the important affairs of life, Ellen would suddenly be moved to arise with her ear-rending "Yip! Yip!" and "career" (I use Miss Sarah's word) across the landscape. Her frocks, because of her mother's dislike to the dull work of letting down tucks and hems, were shorter than those worn in my decorous young days, and her thin little legs measured the distance like a pair of dividers. There was an intensity to her flight that made one think of a projectile.

From the excursions into tenderness that our little quartette of girls was always making, from our sudden flashes of maturity, Ellen would suddenly leap with both feet into full childhood. I remember sudden jumps from high lofts and swinging from trees and the slipping off of shoes and stockings for the purpose of wading in brooks. And these impassioned returns to the golden age were always heightened by the presence of Alec. Such "performances" were, of course, severely criticized. New England at that time was staider than it is to-day; a higher standard of what was named "decorum" was demanded of the young, and yet smiles flickered around mouths while brows frowned when Ellen played.

As I read Ellen's journal at this time, it is as though I could see her growing up as the tide comes in; the receding wave toward childhood meant Alec to her. He was a loosely built lad with a humorous and smiling mouth. His shaggy mane of hair, which boys wore longer in those days than they do now, gave him the appearance of a lion's cub. His whimsical temperament and his easy disposition he got from his mother. She was a placid woman who had spent her life in adapting herself to the difficult temperament of Mr. Yorke, and it was her boast that there was no other woman living who could have got on with her husband without being fidgeted into an early grave. When Miss Sarah opined that if she put her mind on that and on nothing else, she could get on with any man living, Mrs. Yorke replied nothing, but said afterwards to my grandmother:—

"Poor Miss Sarah! Ain't it queer about these unmarried women; no matter how intellectual they be! It ain't puttin' your mind on it ever made a woman get on with the man she's married to."

Whatever the knack was that made a woman accomplish this feat, Alec had had imparted by his mother.

"Learnin' you to get on with your pa real easy an' smilin' is goin' to help you a lot in life, Alec," the good woman had told her son. "Mebbe it'll be worth more to you than as if we had money to leave you."

Understanding the virtues in a good but crotchety and trying man, had bred in Alec a tolerant and humorous spirit of the kind that most people don't ever acquire at all, and that Youth seldom knows. It made him kind to boys younger than himself, and also made it easy for his mother to make him play the part of nurse to smaller brothers and sisters and also to nieces and nephews, for Mrs. Yorke's married sister lived next door to her. It was the constant presence of a small child in Alec's train that made Ellen discover the mystery about him.

"There's a deep mystery about Alec," Ellen told me. "Every day he comes and leaves his baby with me at a certain time and runs off rapidly toward the Butlers'."

Now I had seen Alec Yorke grow up; he was younger than I, and you know the scorn that a girl of thirteen can have toward a boy a year her junior and half a head shorter than she. At that time he fits into no scheme of things; there is no being on earth who arouses one's sentiment less. As a sweetheart he is impossible; equally impossible is he as an object on which to lavish motherly feelings. For me, Alec was a mere plague; he lured Ellen from me into skylarkings in which I had no part, nor did I wish to have, having, by the New England training of that day, already had my childhood taken from me. It was not mystery that I had ever connected with Alec, but a baffling sense of humor and an intensity in the way he could turn hand-springs. There was a fire in his performance of cart-wheels that seemed to let loose all that was foolish and gay, and, from the point of view of the grown-ups of the time, reprehensible in Ellen. So it was obvious to me that any mysterious doings of Alec's meant no good.

"We ought to find out," said I, "what he's about."

"Oh, Roberta!" pleaded Ellen; "then it wouldn't be a mystery any more."

"We ought to find out what he's doing," I pursued, "and get him to stop it. We should use our influence even if he is young."

We, therefore, stealthily made after Alec. He went out through a hole in the fence of the Scudder place, circled a little wood, scaled some outhouses of the Jones's, and in this circuitous method came back to old Mrs. Butler's, next door, and there he lay on his stomach in the woodshed, at a little distance. With a reappearance of guilty stealth, he looked around and seeing no one he dove suddenly into Mrs. Butler's house. Mrs. Butler was stricken with rheumatism and lived entirely on the first floor, so by the simple method of flattening our noses against the window-pane we might find out anything that was afoot. We fathomed the mystery. There stood Alec, doing old Mrs. Butler's back hair. He combed it out as best he might, while she punctuated the performance with such remarks as these: "Lor! child, remember it's hair in your hands, not a hank of yarn." Then she would groan, "Oh, the day that I lost the use of my arms over my head and must go through this!" All of which Alec bore with patience.

We made off a little shamefacedly while Ellen hissed in my ear, with fine logic: "There, Roberta Hathaway, that's what you get by snooping into people's business." We never mentioned Alec's

mystery to him, though from time to time Ellen would seem
maddeningly knowing.

CHAPTER III

When Mrs. Payne had been in our village less than a year and the interest of the village in the "do-less" sister of Miss Sarah had somewhat dwindled, it flamed up again. Mrs. Payne had a visitor, to our country eyes a splendid-looking, middle-aged gentleman. He put up at the little inn and called on Mrs. Payne and brought her such little trifles as a man might bestow upon a lady; sweets also he brought for Ellen, and a most elegant little needlecase with a gold thimble,—an incongruous gift, for since Ellen learned the use of the needle she had abhorred it; if she lived to-day she would have darned her stockings with a sail needle and dental floss. There went through the town, "He's courting the widow," for he came again and again, and in the mean time, according to the postmistress, there arrived letters and a package or two.

Concerning this episode Ellen writes:—

"I wish aunts were made of different stuff. When Aunt Sarah comes down here looking like a gorgon, I know that she has come to make my mother cry and I am very glad that I called her 'old gorgon-face' right before her one time, though it is a rude way to address one's female relatives and I apologized to her afterwards, and now I think I will have to undo my apology because I feel so glad and happy every time I think I called her it. I couldn't help hearing because I was in the next room, and anyway I didn't mind if I did hear it. She said to my mother: 'I suppose you've made up your mind already what to do about Mr. Dennett.' 'About Mr. Dennett?' said my mother, and she sounded frightened,—she is much more frightened of my Aunt Sarah than I am. 'Even you can't be such a ninny,' said my aunt, 'as to think he comes here for nothing. A man of his age doesn't come from Springfield for the purpose of an afternoon's conversation.' 'I hadn't faced it that way,' said mamma. 'Pooh! Pooh!' said my aunt. 'There's a limit to even your folly; I hope you have planned to do the sensible thing and if you have not, you should save him the humiliation of declaring himself, which he'll do now very soon, no doubt.' 'He pretended business brought him here,' said my mother. 'Business, indeed,' said Aunt Sarah, and she made a noise like a snort, which if I made she would consider very rude. I wish there was one day a year when children could tell their aunts how rude they are at times, just as their aunts tell them every day in the week. 'The business of courting is what he is about, and with an atom of honesty you must know it, and now I want to know what you are going to do.' 'It's rather hard; I'm going to call Ellen,' said my mother; and I had to move rather rapidly not to be found too near the door, which showed me that I was listening, which one ought never to do. 'Ellen,' said my mother; and my aunt then said a word which I am not allowed to say. 'Squizzelty Betsey,' said she, 'what has Ellen to do with it?' 'I'm going to consult with Ellen'; and then, when I was in the room, 'Ellen,' she said, 'your aunt seems to think that Mr. Dennett wishes to become a new father to you. How do you like this idea?' 'Would you have to keep house for him,' I said, 'the way you did for dear papa?' 'More so,' said my mamma. 'I don't think we should be happy then,' said I. At this Aunt Sarah rocked back and forth and she groaned as though her stomach hurt her. While my aunt was groaning, I could see my mother turn her back and I knew by her actions that she was putting her handkerchief to her mouth to keep from laughing, and which I have often seen her do when my aunt was here. 'It made us both very nervous,' I explained to her, 'getting meals exactly on time and doing all the things that a man has a right to have perfect in his own house, which is what papa used to say, but we have not, since we've lived together, had to have anything perfect at all; we never think of meal-times or any other sad things.' 'Listen, Ellen,' said my aunt; 'you are almost more sensible and grown-up than your mother; your mother is still a young woman, a long life of loneliness confronts her,—more than that, a cramped financial situation. You'll always have to go without and without and without. It would be from every point of view a dignified and suitable alliance and one which your mother should be happy to make and which any woman of her age and position and an atom of sense would do.' Here my mother flung out her hand in the air as though she were throwing away something and were glad to do it. I wish I could see her do that again. 'I respect him and I like him, and his liking for me touches me and flatters me, but oh! the running of a big house; but oh! the pent-up city streets.' 'And I say so, too,' I cried. Then she suddenly drew me to her and stood me at arm's length from her, and she said to me, 'Ellen, promise me when you grow up, and when your blood shall leap high, and nothing happens in this little town, and when the world calls to you, that you won't blame me.' And my aunt said, 'Don't worry, Emily; plenty will always happen where Ellen is.' I hugged and kissed her and promised hard. Now there will be no more presents, and no more bon-bons, for mother is going to shock him so he will not want to come again, which she thinks is a good way to save his vanity, but Aunt Sarah said: 'Emily, you are incorrigible.' But we are both, my mother and I, very sorry to lose our good friend. 'Can't men be friends with you,' I asked, 'without wanting to marry you?' And my mother said, 'It seems not, dear.' But when I grow up it is going to be different with me."

CHAPTER IV

Ellen wrote about this time:—

"Grandma Hathaway, Aunt Sarah and mamma, all don't know what to do about me. I should be much grown-upper than I am. 'Mercy,' said Aunt Sarah, 'that great girl of yours, Emily, acts so that she makes me tremble for fear she will some day swing by a tail from a bough, like a monkey.' [Here we see Miss Grant foreshadowing the Darwinian theory.] They don't know I try to be good, but I do try; but when joy gets into my feet I have to run, and I love to feel like that. I think I only try to be good when I am not happy. I have said my prayers about it, and the awful thing is when I say my prayers I feel as if God said: 'Never mind, Ellen, run if you like.' They always say to me: 'Why can't you sit and sew under the trees with the other girls?' Oh, if they only knew what we talked about when we sit and sew! And even Roberta does, though she disapproves of all silliness. I have never seen any girl disapprove of all silliness as does Roberta. But what we sit and talk about is beaux, though Roberta doesn't call hers that, and he isn't. And when Roberta talks so beautifully, I often talk the same way, but deep in my heart I know I wish I had a real beau, like the grown-up girls we talk about. It's strange, though, that Roberta has none, because she has more of one than any of the rest of us, because she writes notes to Leonard Dilloway and he carries home her books. When I said, 'He is your beau,' she was very shocked. 'I wish you would not speak so to me,' she said, 'it pains me. I shall never love, anyway, but once. I am far too young to think of such things.' 'Why do you do it?' I asked her. This made her cross. 'I don't,' she answered. 'Leonard is my friend.' But the rest of us know she is in love. So when they talk to me about being a hoyden and ask me to sit and sew, I feel like a hypocrite, because I know that young girls like us are much more grown-up than they were when Aunt Sarah and Grandma Hathaway were young, and that they would dislike one as much as the other. Though I am young in actions I have such old thoughts that I am surprised and wish I could help being proud of myself for them. I have older thoughts than Janie or Mildred, or even Roberta. Roberta sounds older, but her thoughts are tied with strings while mine are not."

This sketch of hers is an accurate picture of the conversations between young girls that are going on forever and ever when three or four long-legged youngsters are together. Their talk leads inevitably, as did ours, toward their business in life. To the lads we were adventures—not to be confused with the real business they had to do in the world; to us they were life itself.

Like all young girls, we lived in a close little world of our own. No one entered it, nor could we come out toward others'. We were passionate spectators at the feast of life, picking up the crumbs of experience which came our way; for in our civilization we are treated as children at an age when Juliet ran away for love, and Beatrice set Dante's heart to beating. And yet our hearts beat, and we were tragic and ineffectual Juliets, appearing on our balconies to youths who saw only the shortness of our skirts. We knew without knowing that our little lean arms were to be the cradles of the unborn generation. Forever and ever we tried to tell those whom we met, "I am Eve," and couldn't, not knowing the way past the angel with the flaming sword of self-consciousness.

It was the great adventure of Janie Acres which made us conscious of our absorption in boys. There had been a merry-making which took place in a barn, and in talking it over afterwards, we recounted the conversation of each boy who had spoken to us, giving the impression of having snubbed them one and all; which, indeed, we often did, but against our wills, because embarrassment made us gruff.

Janie had the adventure of hiding in the same corn-bin with a lad, and what occurred in the corn-bin she was coy of telling. When pressed, she flushed and looked the other way. It was Ellen who brought the utter innocence and lack of romance to light with her merciless truthfulness.

"Did he kiss you?" asked she.

We were shocked at her frankness. We never spoke of such things as kisses directly. The delicacy of our little souls was deeply wounded.

And Janie replied:—

"Well, not exactly. But," she faltered, "he would have if I had stayed there."

"How do you know?" asked Ellen coldly.

Thus it was she pricked the bubble of sentiment. We were all rather horrified, immensely interested and rather envious. We now perceived our sentimentality. We ourselves were shocked a little by some of our temerities, for in the wide conspiracy of silence around us we imagined we were the only adventurous ones in the world. Characteristically, it was I who suggested that momentous association, the "Zinias," or "Old Maid Club."

Ellen wrote:—

"We made up our minds that we were always to be true friends of men and lift their minds up as women should. We are going to think only of our studies, our homes, and of religion. Roberta says we may as well begin now, for we are getting older every minute, and one of us is already fourteen. And before we know it we will be thinking of nothing but boys. We have only to look around us to see what such things lead to. Patty Newcomb and Elizabeth Taylor and all those big girls are both forward and bold. When I said, 'Roberta, isn't noticing everything they do and talking about it just the same as talking about boys?' she said at once, 'It is not the same at all,' in the tone that I know she doesn't want me to say anything more. And when I said, 'Oh, Roberta, aren't we rather young yet to think about being old maids?' she replied sternly, 'It is never too young to begin.'"

I feel rather sorry now for the stern, little Roberta. I feel sorry, too, for Janie Acres and her kiss that never was. She would have been so proud of it; it would have been her proof that she was a young lady.

CHAPTER V

No sooner had Ellen covenanted "Thou shalt not!" than off she went on her first adventure,—a trifling one but bleeding. She walked one day to the academy with Arthur McLain. He wore long trousers. Of this fatal occurrence Ellen remarks touchingly: "I tried very hard to be interesting, but I chose the wrong thing." It is a mistake frequently made by grown men and women. Alas! capricious fate that governs these things turned my sweet, unconscious Ellen to one forever on the alert for the appearance of this long-legged quidnunc.

I will give three or four paragraphs from her journal:—

"I asked Aunt Sarah if she wanted me to get her some more yarn when hers ran short. She answered, 'Yes, you may, though I wish, Ellen, my dear child, that you were as eager to do your work as you are to wait on others.' But I knew all the time that I offered to go because I hoped that I should see him, and I should have told my aunt that that was why I offered."

A few days later comes the touching little expression of the desire of the eyes:—

"Last week I walked all over town to catch glimpses of him. I went to the post-office, and he wasn't there; I went down past the school-house and past his house, and whenever I saw a boy coming toward me, it was hard to breathe. The whole day was empty and I thought it would never be night."

Again:—

"To-day I saw him; he passed by me and just said, 'Hulloa, Ellen.' When I stopped for a moment, I thought he would speak to me. In school this morning he stopped and talked, but all my words went away and I seemed so stupid. At night I make up things I would like to say to him, and when he stops for a moment,—oh, he stops so seldom,—I forget them all."

Throughout all this, not once does she use the word love. From that terrible and impersonal longing, unaware of itself and unrecognized, Ellen walked out toward the long-trousered boy. She spread before him as much as she could of her little shy sweetnesses. She walked up and down the silent streets waiting for him. Later she writes: "I had no single reason in the world for liking him."

I was with Ellen at the moment of her disillusion. We were out walking together when Arthur McLain came toward us. Ahead of us, tail wagging, ran the beloved mongrel Faro. He stopped to sniff at Arthur. Arthur shooed him away. He was a lad timid about dogs, it seems. Faro saw his nervousness, and, for deviltry, barked. Arthur kicked at him with the savageness of fear.

I can see Ellen now gathering her dog to her with one regal sweep of the hand and walking past the boy, her head erect, her cheeks scarlet.

"I hate a coward," she said to me in a low, tense voice; and later with a flaming look, "I would have killed him with my hands if he had hurt Faro," she cried.

So humiliated was she that she says no word in her journal for her reason for her change of heart. She could not forgive him for having made a fool of herself about him—about one so unworthy. For of all things in the world hard to forgive, this is the hardest.

"I would be glad if he were dead. Oh, I know I am awful, but it is like that. Think of him walking around this town day by day, and I will have to meet him; when I go uptown, when I go to school, I will be avoiding him exactly the way I used to look for him. Oh, if he would only go away."

It is not only Ellen who would like to slay the dead ghosts of unworthy loves.

"He walks up and down, and doesn't know I have looked at him. Oh, if he knew that, I think I should die [her journal goes on]. He walks up and down and doesn't know that I so hate the sight of him. I don't hate him, but just the sight of him—so awfully I hate it. Everything he does seems to me so tiresome; his loud laugh makes me feel sick, and he doesn't know anything. I make-believe to myself that he walked all over town after me and got in my way and annoyed me until I said, 'I will be very glad, Arthur, if you would cease these undesired attentions.' How could he cease anything he had never begun, for it wasn't at all like that it happened. I should feel so much happier if I only could have hurt him, too."

This experience, so phantasmal and yet so poignant, led to the Zinias' premature death. Conscience invaded Ellen now that disillusion had done its blighting work. There came a day when she could no longer keep to herself her deviation from the precise morals demanded by the Zinias.

It was after a walk toward evening up the mountain, full of pregnant silences, that she confessed:—

"You would despise me, if you really knew me. I'm not the kind of a girl we are trying to be."

It shocked me and thrilled me at the same time.

"What have you been doing?" I asked her.

"I can't tell you," she told me. "You would despise me too much."

"Why, Ellen!" I cried. "Tell me about it."

"No! No!" she said; and she buried her face in the moss in a very agony of shame. "I can't tell a human soul."

And she still left me with a feeling of having had an interesting sentimental experience. Thus may we, when young, rifle sweetness from the blossom of despair.

It was communicated to the other two Zinias that Ellen's

conduct had been unbecoming a sincere old maid, and when they turned on her, instead of shame, she had for them: "I hate your society, anyway! I never did want to be an old maid!"

As I look back, this adventure closes for us a certain phase of life as definitely as though we had shut the door. We all realized, though we were not honest enough to say it aloud, that we too didn't wish to be old maids. And all this happened because an unlovable boy had made Ellen like him. So much at the mercy of men are women! Just a shadow of the Cyprian over us and we blossomed. It was the shadow of a shadow; it had not one little objective event to give it substance, yet the Zinias withered.

CHAPTER VI

With a deep revulsion of feeling, Ellen gave up girls, sewing, and Zinias, and made a dash into childhood with Alec Yorke. Alec at this time was a strong lad of thirteen, a head shorter than Ellen. I remember even then he seemed more a person than the other boys, though at the monkey-shining age.

They egged one another on until the ordinary obstacles that stand in people's way did not exist. They became together drunken with the joy of life. In this mood, they disappeared together one day, to the scandal of Miss Sarah. She was particularly annoyed because Mrs. Payne refused to be disturbed by the event.

"While he and Ellen are off together, they are somewhere having a good time. Why should I worry?" said she. They had come together to find out if Ellen was at my house.

"If I had known Ellen was gone with Alec, Sarah, I should never have gone to look for her. I wasn't worried about her, anyway; I only wanted company," said she, with more asperity than usual.

The two returned at sunset, the glamour of a glorious day about them. They merely told vaguely: "They had been off on the mountain."

It leaked out that they had been as far as the village, ten miles away, and that the peddler had given them a lift back. This last was a scandal.

An Irish peddler lived on the outskirts of our village, and this was before the day when foreigners were plenty. He lived contrary to our American customs,—the pig roamed at will, in friendly fashion, through his cabin. He sang in Gaelic as he drove his cart with its moth-eaten, calico horse,—songs that were now wildly sad, now wildly gay. He was alien, so we disapproved of him.

I remonstrated with Ellen on this.

"I like him," was her only answer.

This had not been all the adventure, nor was this the end of it. To tell the story in Ellen's own words:—

"Alec and I were picking currants at Aunt Sarah's when I heard a voice behind me, and I never knew before what it meant when I read in books, that 'their hearts were in their mouths.' I thought mine would beat its way right out of me and lie thumping at my feet when I heard a voice say: 'Oh, here are my little friends from Erin's Isle.' I suppose it is because I am very bad that it never occurred to me until that minute that fooling a minister, by pretending to be the peddler's children, was not right, especially when it was Alec's and my singing songs in what we made him believe was Gaelic that made him buy so many more things. I wonder if all people who do wrong only feel badly when they are found out? I turned around and I thought I should fall, for my mother was with him, and Aunt Sarah and uncle and our own minister. Uncle Ephraim had not heard what he said, and now, 'Permit me, Mr. Sweetser,' he said, 'to present my little niece, Ellen, Mrs. Payne's little daughter, and our neighbor, Master Alec Yorke.' I saw him wondering if we really could be the same children, because, while we were playing that we were the peddler's children, we had taken off our shoes and stockings to make ourselves look like wild Irish children, and had succeeded very well, indeed. I thought for a moment that perhaps he wouldn't say anything, but Aunt Sarah's ears were open. 'What was that? Did I hear you say "your little friends from Erin"? Have you seen these children before?' This was an awful moment. 'These are the same children that came with the Irish peddler to my house.' 'Ha! Ha! I knew that those children were gone for no good, Emily, and that they were strangely silent about their exploits,' Aunt Sarah said. 'Do you mean,' said Uncle Ephraim, 'that my niece and Horace Yorke's son made believe to be the children of a drunken, Irish peddler, and thus appeared before you?' 'Not only that,' said Mr. Sweetser sadly, 'but they sang to us in Gaelic.' 'Gaelic,' snorted Aunt Sarah; 'never a word does she know of Gaelic. I have heard her making up gibberish to the tunes that that peddler sings on his way.' Here Alec acted extremely noble, though it annoyed me very much, and I am sure that I am a very ungrateful girl that it did annoy me. He spoke right up and said: 'Mr. Grant, it is all my fault. It was I who thought of being children of the Irish peddler and I who suggested that we hop on his cart. I should take all the blame.' There was not one word of truth in this, for we had often ridden with the peddler before, and the idea of playing that we were his children was my own, and without thinking I told them so. 'Let us say no more about this childish prank,' said Mr. Sweetser. 'These children have shown real nobility, the little lad in desiring to shield Miss Ellen and Miss Ellen in not permitting herself to be shielded.' Well, I knew that we should have more of it and plenty later, and we did when Aunt Sarah came ravening—there is no other word to use for it, though I know it is not polite—down to our house. It all oppressed me very much, even though Alec whispered: 'We can make-believe we are being persecuted by the Philistines.' I know I have disgraced the family, but I shall never understand why riding with the peddler should do this. If our family is any good, it should take more than this. Uncle Ephraim and Aunt Sarah have said that I am really too old to act as I do. When I answer, 'But if I act so, doesn't it show that I am not too old, Aunt Sarah?' she says: 'Mercy, my child, as tall as any flagpole and with legs like a beanstalk, you've got to be acting like a young lady. We can't have young women of our family getting a ridiculous name.' This means that I must give up Alec. 'Why you want that child around all the time is incomprehensible to me,' said my aunt. 'You are a good head higher than he is.' People are always measuring things in length and breadth. How can one measure one's friends by the pound? Roberta agrees with them. She thinks I am giddy, and feels that she must be good for me. I love Roberta more than any other earthly being beside mamma, but when Roberta tries to be good for me, I am so

wicked that I try to be bad for Roberta, and can very easily
be so."

This episode stopped the free skylarking with Alec. As you
have seen, it was explained to Ellen that since she was fourteen and
nearly a young lady, she must behave as such. When I think how
many lovely spontaneities have been offered on the sad and drab
altar of young ladyhood, I could weep, as Ellen did. Alec's
suggestion that they were being persecuted by the Philistines did
not comfort her, and little Mrs. Payne said sadly:—

"Your aunt and uncle are right, Ellen, and I suppose I'll have to
punish you to satisfy them, but I can't help knowing that you must
have had a perfectly wonderful day, and they are few in this world.
Don't let your punishment cloud your memory."

CHAPTER VII

Look back and see if you can remember when it was you drifted from that part of the river of life that is little girlhood to that time when you recognized that you were grown up, and the eyes of men rested on you speculatively, interestedly, and your parents foreshadowed these things by an irritating watchfulness that you did not understand. The picture of Ellen that comes to me oftenest is one of her progress through the streets, her hair in an anguished neatness, from her desire to escape Miss Sarah's critical censure, her skirts longer now, and behind her perpetually screeled the three motherless babes of our not long widowed minister. He was a middle-aged man, ineffectual except for some occasional Gottbetrunkener moments. From my present vantage-point I now recognize him to be one of the brothers of St. Francis by temperament. He had a true poetic sense, and Ellen would go to his house for the purpose of washing dishes and helping about, performing her labors with the precision which she had only for the work of other people, her own room, to my anguish, being a whited sepulcher of disorder, outwardly fair to the glance of her Aunt Sarah, while dust lay thick in every unobservable spot. It was I who kept her bureau drawers in order.

She writes:—

"I just can't waste a minute indoors. I don't know why grown people have so many things to do. When I get married I am going to live in a tent and have just one cupboard where I keep everything, with doors that can't be seen through. Roberta wrings her hands, but she would wring them more if she knew that I have from earliest childhood learned to sleep quietly in my bed as it takes less time to make it when I get up. And mother doesn't care one bit more than I. I am so glad. She so frequently says: 'Ellen, this is too sweet a day to cook'; and we eat bread and milk all day, and don't even light the stove, though there have been moments when I have been glad that there is a big kitchen in which they are always cooking, up at my Aunt Sarah's. We would get things done much better if it were not for reading aloud, but so frequently mother finds things she wants to read, and then we go on, but not on and on like Mr. Sylvester and I. We began reading poetry the other day—how shall I tell it? And he read and I read, and he read and I read, until we understood everything we were reading, the very heart. We felt as if we had made the poetry—just knowing it for ourselves, and it was us. By pretending I am Mr. Sylvester's second wife sent by the Lord to take care of his motherless children, I find I can do housework very well, for me, though I feel rather guilty when I look at him, for I know that even he might be exasperated at the thought of me as his second wife. But one has to do something."

Some weeks later this occurs:—

"Now I have learned to work so beautifully and have done so well, besides taking care of the children and then baking, I feel it isn't fair not to do it at home. Oh, how hard it is to do work for one's self. I know I should think I am doing it for my mother, and when I was very little I used to pretend that I was a poor child who supported her mother; but the little silly pretenses of childhood are now impossible for me since I am so much over fifteen."

It was at this time that we began to be allowed to go to the young people's parties, because with us there was no fixed and rigid time when girls come out. They went when their legs were long enough and when they had learned to fold their hands properly in their laps and sit with decorum, which with Ellen and myself occurred somewhere toward sixteen. Ellen writes of one of these parties:—

"I am sitting waiting to go. I have a new pale-blue dress with little ruffles—little, tiny ruffles. Aunt Sarah is disgusted that mother put so much work into my dress because it isn't practical, when we need so many things, for her to waste her eyes. And it is true, but oh, how much more fun it is to work on ornaments than useful things, and parties are like ornaments. I think they are like jewels, and a great, big, enormous party, with lights and flowers, like one reads about in books, must be like having strings of pearls. All I hope is that I will act politely, and not show how pleased I am, because if I did I should shout and sing. My Aunt Sarah said: 'Ellen, please, my child, don't make me feel as if you were going to burst into flame or perhaps slide down the banisters.' And, indeed, I often look in the glass and wonder that I can look so quiet and unshining."

It was in this high mood that Ellen met Edward Graham. I know now that he must have been an honest lad, square-cornered, solid, with an awkward, bearish, honest walk, nice, kind eyes, and a short mop of wiry, glinting curls as his only beauty, which fitted his head like a close-clinging cap, stopping abruptly instead of straggling down unkemptwise, as hair is apt to do, on the back of his neck and temples. It was Ellen who noticed this and wrote about it. He must have been not over one-and-twenty, but he was instructor at the academy in chemistry and mathematics.

Well do I remember hearing this conversation at the other side of a vine-trellis at this party. In her low, pensive voice Ellen was saying: "I lived by the sea; it was in my veins. The noise of its beating is in my heart. One cannot live inland when one has been a lighthouse-keeper's daughter."

Rage and anger surged in me, for Ellen had made but three visits to the sea in all her days, and one of which occurred when she was too small to remember it. As you may gather from this, her father had not been a lighthouse-keeper. I stamped my foot; a little-girl mad feeling came over me. I took my saucer of goodies and my cake firmly in my hand and went to confront her then and there. She had talked so beautifully about truth and life that very afternoon.

I couldn't do it. The little sarcastic remark that anger had invented for me died still-born. She was too lovely; something almost mystically beautiful radiated from her whole little personality. "I am so happy," she seemed to say. "Let me stay happy one moment more." There was always about her this heart-rending quality. It was not until I could draw her by herself that I spoke to her, and then my remonstrance was gentle.

"You must tell him the truth," I insisted kindly.

And Ellen wrung her hands and said:—

"Oh, Roberta! you make my heart feel like a shriveled-up little leaf; you make me feel like a bad dream, like when you find yourself in company without your clothes."

But I repeated inexorably:—

"You must tell him."

I can see her now drooping up to him and the appealing glance of her large eyes. Presently I saw him take both her hands in his, and then she came toward me, her feet dancing, a glad, naughty look in her eyes. She answered my glance of inquiry with:—

"He asked me why I told him what I did, and, since I was telling the whole truth, I answered, 'I wanted awfully to have you like me.'"

That, you see, is what I got for interfering with my friend and torturing her.

CHAPTER VIII

The next few weeks there were very few entries.

Ellen was very bad at mathematics, and her uncle, who rarely left his seclusion to interest himself in her affairs and who merely enjoyed her personality, thought it would be a fine plan if this responsible young man should give his Ellen lessons. Mr. Grant was advanced in his theories concerning the female brain, which, he said, lost its vagueness and inexactnesses through a mathematical training. Ellen merely makes a note of this.

There are very few entries in her journal at this time, for she was playing with the great forces of life. God help us all! We didn't know passion when it came to us, nor how should we? It was the warp on which were woven all our generous impulses, all our high idealisms, making in all the shimmering garments in which we clothed our fragile, newborn spirits.

Ellen walked in a magic circle of her own ignorance, never dreaming of love or of being in love. So absorbed was she that it seemed like some one walking down a road that leads directly into a swift-flowing river, and not knowing that the river was there until one had walked directly into it. So close is the so-called silly moment of girlhood to the moment of full development, that when the change comes it sometimes takes only overnight. It was only a few pages, after all, that separated Ellen, who managed to do the minister's dishes by pretending that she was his second wife, from the Ellen who wrote:—

"I don't know how to begin what I am going to say. I thought everybody in the world must know what had happened to me. I thought my face must shine with it. I thought I must look like some one very different from myself,—like a woman, perhaps. I came home through Lincoln Field and squeezed myself through a hole in the fence so no one could see me. I came up the back way to my room and locked the door. My heart beat both ways at once when I looked in the glass, but I looked just the same as before I went out—as before he kissed me. I went downstairs and my hand seemed too heavy to open the door and go in where I heard their voices. I was afraid to go because I felt: 'They will know, they will know!' Mr. Sylvester and mamma and Aunt Sarah were there. 'Where have you been?' said mamma. And I could not answer. I felt I had been gone so long and so far. I could hear the blood beating in my ears, and when my aunt said: 'I wish, Ellen, you would stand up straighter,' I could hardly lift my head."

Next day there is an entry: "I didn't know we were engaged until he told me, 'Why, of course, we are.'"

Thus simply does youth plight its troth. They had been together and he had kissed her, and so, of course, they were engaged. Of course, they were ready to fight the long battle of life side by side, and she who had given so much in her kiss had walked out past the doors of girlhood; through that one light touch she felt that her whole life must be then surrendered to the boy who had had the magic word for her. They decided to tell no one on account of their youth.

No sooner did this honest lad have my rainbow Ellen in his hands than he started in trying to make some one else of her. I read her journal that follows with a certain heartache because I was not blameless in this matter. I, too, wanted to take this gay and shimmering child and turn her into something else; trim her generosities and check her impulses.

Another thing that makes me rage is the fact that my knowledge of the lives of men teaches me that, had Ellen had one little affectation in which to clothe herself, her young lover would have been on his knees before her instead of being the pedantic young master. Ellen's journal at this time varies from a thing glittering with life, from being drunk with the heady wine of being beloved for the first time, to a book of copy-book maxims, beginning with: "Edward says I must read—or do—or act—or mustn't."

Poor young man! He wrote her decalogues by the dozen, and

yet the tragedy of him is that he tasted her special quality and loved her while trying to kill it. The youth of Ellen and her high joy of living carried him along in spite of himself, though he always made Ellen pay for his happiness by lectures on the seriousness of life.

It was here that Alec began to perceive the place he had in her life. They had a game they played that they called "Two Years Ago," in which they outdid their own childish pranks. Ellen remarks ingenuously:—

> "I suppose that I ought to tell Edward how Alec and I rest ourselves from growing up, but there is no place in him to tell this to. I tried it with Roberta, and she just understood what it was about, but doesn't see why I want to do it; and I don't know myself exactly, except that I just have to."

Then from one day to another Alec was sent West to an uncle and two weeks later, as had been planned, Edward left. He was to go away for a year and a half, and then come back and formally ask for Ellen's hand. It shocked Ellen terribly that she missed Alec most.

Through all the year and a half that followed, Ellen never told me anything of what was in her mind, nor did she tell her mother, and here is the characteristic of their young girlhood that people seem to forget—this nameless reticence. So, alone, she went through the crucial thing that falling out of love always is. Another girl in her situation might have deceived herself, the idea of a grown-up lover was such a pleasant one to a girl of Ellen's age. Ellen was unaware of the disillusion she was preparing for herself. She writes, appalled:—

> "I don't know what has happened to me, I can only describe it by saying I have waked up. I know now that I am not in love with Edward and I just understood this from one day to another. He has not done anything at all. He writes me just the way he always has. He hasn't changed, so I suppose I am fickle and bad, and that I can't trust myself, for if this wasn't real, I don't know what can

be real, and yet I feel as though I had never loved him at all. I sometimes wonder if I should have become engaged to some other person if it had happened that some other person had kissed me."

Write him of her change of heart she could not, for as time went on apparently the memory of her became dearer to the boy. Good and slow and pedantic, he yet realized what a lovely thing life had put into his hands, and he longed to keep it, and he communicated this ever-growing longing to Ellen. She so wanted to keep faith with herself and to live up to all the things about "one love and only one love" that books from all time have taught young girls they ought to feel. She felt a great need of talking about it with some one and could not bring herself to do it.

"If I could only tell some one and ask what to do, but it seems disloyal. Roberta wouldn't understand and some way I don't want to worry my little mother. Sometimes I feel as if I did tell her without saying any words, when I sit beside her and hold her hand and feel afraid. The other night we sat alone in the dark. The smell of honeysuckle vines was so sweet that I shall never smell it again without thinking how soft her hand felt in the dark. She said: 'When I was your age, I used often to want to tell my mother things and didn't dare. My mother was more like your Aunt Sarah.' My heart beat so when she said this that it seemed as if she could hear it, but I only pressed her hand and kissed it. Then she said to me: 'You have seemed a little absent-minded lately, my darling child; have you anything on your mind, Ellen?' And I said in a low voice, and blushing,—and I took my face off her hand for fear she would feel me blush against it,—'What should I have?'"

As I read her cramped little handwriting a sudden wave of shame creeps over me as though I had gone back; I remember her so well; I was so on the outside; I loved her so truly. Meantime, as every day shortened the distance that separated them, a certain dread encompassed Ellen; she visualized their approach one to another in this way:—

"It was as if I was standing still and he was standing still, and that the space between us was being shortened by little jerks, and each jerk was as a day that makes us come nearer and nearer. I don't want to see him—oh, I don't want to see him. I don't know what I'm going to say to him—perhaps nothing. He will look at me kindly—oh, kindly and critically,—and then I shall be afraid; afraid of hurting him—afraid of him."

A little later she writes again:—

"If I go on feeling undecided as to what I shall do, something will snap inside my head. I can't feel so uncertain. He wrote to me lately, 'Ellen, my life would be utterly worthless without you.' I cannot ruin any one's life, and my life is pretty worthless, anyway, so I am going to stand by my first promise, which is the only brave thing to do. Now that I have decided that, I feel at peace. I loved him once and my love will come back."

She adds touchingly, "I have two weeks before he comes"; but these two weeks of respite were denied her. I was going down to Ellen's when I met Edward Graham on his way there also.

"I've come to surprise Ellen," he said. So it happened that it was I who went to her with the words, "Edward Graham's waiting for you downstairs," and wondered at the sudden ebb of color from her face.

CHAPTER IX

It was with her mind utterly made up as to what course to take that she went to her ordeal. She was going to offer herself a little, white offering before the altar of the fetish which decrees that we shall keep our promises. Herding her to this doom were all the cruel things which we teach our young girls. In New England in my day we did not joke about engagements. In her innocence, having given her lover her mouth to be kissed and her hand to be held, and having promised to be his, she had definitely decided that in the sight of God she was his, and so she dressed herself in her best that she might please him.

I suppose that had I made up my mind to do what Ellen did at that age, I should have gone through to the iniquitous end, shut my eyes and quieted my rebellious spirit with sophistries. I should have done according to whichever part of the strange anomalous teaching which we give young girls that I believed in most. Had I believed most that it is the crime of crimes to marry without love, I should have frankly made up my mind to break the engagement, but had I believed that one may love but once, and that an engagement is a marriage of the spirit, and that in giving this I had given so much to one man that I had nothing left for any other,—it is strange, but this is still taught to girls to-day,—I should have traveled that terrible road. For girls as young as Ellen have to find their way around through a world that is hung with a cobweb of lies, which is put there to screen us from the real world. The suffering that the unlearning of these lies has given to girls of our class from all time is greater than the suffering through which we must pass to come to a wider religious belief.

Ellen might make up her mind as to what to do, but she lived by instincts. She writes about it:—

"I couldn't. All day I pretended to myself that I was glad he was coming, and that as soon as I saw him everything would be all right, but it is a terrible, awful thing. He cares. He put his arms out toward me and said:

'Ellen, oh, Ellen!' All I could say—I was so cruel, so stupid—was, 'Don't, don't'; and I meant I didn't want him to touch me. And then he said, and it was worse because he has grown much older looking, 'I don't understand. What's the matter, Ellen?' I said, 'I can't marry you; I don't love you.' He said: 'Why, what have I done?' What could I tell him? It was just that he was he and I was I, and that's no reason, and yet it is the only reason in the world that you can't change, and that's why you love people and that's why you don't love them. We both stood and just stared at each other. While I looked at him all the color went out of his face and it grew gray. 'When did it happen, Ellen?' he said. 'I don't know,' I told him; 'it just went out.' 'You might have told me.' 'I meant never to tell you,' I said; and then his color all came back to his face and this was worse than before. 'You meant to marry me just the same? Then you do care for me; it's just an idea you've gotten; it's just because we have been apart so long. Let's just go on just as you meant to, Ellen, if there is no one else.' He opened his arms as if he wanted to hide me from myself in them, but I don't know what happened to me. I just said, 'No-no-no-no,' and ran out of the room, and out of the house up into the orchard. I didn't notice, but threw myself down under the tree and cried and cried. I don't know how long I was there, but I heard my mother saying: 'Ellen, Ellen,' and the sound of her footsteps coming toward me, but I couldn't stop sobbing so that she wouldn't find me like that. She heard me and came to me and said, 'Why, Ellen darling! Child, it is as wet as a river here.' She felt my dress and at first it seemed to me that it must be wet with my tears, but it was just the grass. 'What is it, Ellen?' she said to me, and I told her that we had been engaged and that I had just seen Edward, and told him that I didn't want to marry him; and she just folded me in her arms and said, 'Why, darling, you needn't'; and she comforted me, and I felt all safe from everything and just like a very little girl. Not many people can feel like that with their mothers, but I don't think unless you can that your mother's a mother to you really. I couldn't go on feeling safe and rested forever. I've broken faith with myself. I can't count on myself any more. It's a terrible thing not to be able to count on people you love, but it's worse not to be able to count on yourself. I couldn't do what I thought was right; how do I know I will be able to keep from doing what's wrong? I think I will try and give up being good, because most of the things people think are good I don't understand why. I might have saved myself all that suffering and been happy and low-minded, comfortable and contented, and I think I will be from now on."

I well remember this epoch in Ellen's life; she must have been between eighteen and nineteen when she gave up hope of herself and went out to be comfortable, low-minded, and happy, for she told me about this spiritual change in her. It was a crisis with Ellen, a spiritual crisis as important as the time in a boy's life when he makes a breach in the "Thou Shalt Nots" that have guarded him around, and surrenders himself to the heady wine of living and says to himself: "I am a sinner; now let's see what there is in sin."

Just about the time Ellen broke her engagement, a boy named Landry lay heavily on my conscience. At this time, also, Ellen was engaged and yet was unhappy, and yet all I knew about Ellen was that there was something weighing heavily on her mind, and all she knew about me was my outward principles in this matter and none of my inward storm and stress. I can remember very well the never-ending conversations we had at this time. I suppose all young girls who are not on terms of familiarity with their own souls thus cloak their real feelings from each other. For there is happily nothing more usual than that shivering, shrinking, spiritual modesty which can tell of no event in life that implicates another human being. Later the weaker women outgrow it shamefully, or the finer ones among us replace it with a beautiful frankness. There are some happy girls who have been so simply brought up that they have never felt the need for the ambiguities of life as Ellen and myself did. The facts of the case were these: Released from the torturing thought of Edward Graham, the breath of life blew through Ellen in a storm, while I was being discreetly courted by George Landry. I had never had a tumultuous suitor, on account of my being matter-of-fact in my attitude toward the boys I knew or instinctively withdrawing myself from any sentimental approach. But now this sentimentally inclined youth had called on me and shown a recurring disposition to try and hold my hand when we were alone together. We read a great deal of poetry also and with deep emphasis. Thus does Satan trick the unwary. I, Roberta, the straightforward; I, the hater of philandering, and who sincerely felt that a self-respecting woman should be proposed to only by a man she would willingly accept as her husband, read verses far-gazing at distant horizons and with gentle underscorings whose audacity set my heart to beating. That I had gone into this slow-moving and decorous little flight of sentiment seemed so contrary to my ideals that I felt I must give up my friend and his poetry-reading and forego the heart-throbbing performance of having my hand gently captured and as gently withdrawing it again, both of us apparently blankly unaware of the actions of our respective hands. Ellen and I would discuss our affairs in ambiguities like this:—

"There's a doom threatening me," Ellen would confess.

"A doom?" asked I, impressed by the sinister darkness of the word.

"Fate has tangled up my life," Ellen averred. "I have been deceived in myself, and now that I know what I am, I don't care."

"What sort of fate?" I then made bold to ask.

"One that will influence my whole life because it has made me glad I'm not good like I tried to be. I love the feeling of having gotten rid of goodness, Roberta"; and Ellen flashed me the smile of a naughty angel, and turned from me to wipe the nose of the youngest Sylvester baby, Prudentia, who accompanied us on our woodsy rambles. "Can you always decide everything in your life?"

"Indeed I cannot," I answered quickly. "I must give up a thing that's sweetest and dearest in life to me, and I can't decide to do it— I am not strong."

"Oh, Roberta!" Ellen cried out. "You are so much stronger than I, for I decided and did the opposite thing."

"What did you want to do?"

"The thing I did do," poor Ellen cried, tears welling up to her sweet eyes. "I wanted to do what I wanted to do, and yet before I so wanted to do what was right." Then, with her little fists pounding on the moss on which we were sitting, she said: "And mighty often, Roberta Hathaway, what people want to do seems to me the really right thing to do."

As I grow older, it seems to me so very often that what people want is really the right thing. There are so many needless sacrifices made in life,—sacrifices that do good to no one and cripple and maim one.

I might have saved myself the worry of giving up the "sweetest and dearest thing in life," for I had an experience which showed me what a solemn young fool I was.

If Ellen and I had this intense spiritual modesty, Janie Acres was not so afflicted. She was always prolific in detail of any sentimental adventure which she had, and was generally only quiet when she had nothing to tell. Ellen summed this characteristic up in her observation on Janie's character:—

"When Roberta and I don't say anything it is because we have too much to say, but when Janie acts as if she knew how God made the world, it is a sure sign she has nothing to tell."

Poor Janie Acres! Through all this long stretch of years I can see her perpetually heart-hungry, wishing for experiences her very eagerness denied her; longing for sympathy, companionship, and love, and when such things came her way, killing them. She had a curious jealousy which was kept from its full bloom by her confidence in herself. When Janie hadn't sufficient sentimental experiences she would invent them. And it was because of her inventions that my little experience which I was taking so seriously was turned to ashes before me.

This trait of Janie's was an incredible one to me. I, who so diligently hid all trace of any sentiment in my life, could never comprehend a temperament that would not only share all its secrets with its friends, but who also invented them; and it was only when Janie had repeatedly emphasized George Landry's attentions to her at moments when I had been reading poetry with him that I realized this. I listened with the gravest feeling of superiority to Janie's artless prattle. If George Landry walked up the street with her, it was an event. I think if she had refused to have him accompany her to a Sunday-School picnic she would have recounted it to us as the refusal of a proposal of marriage.

In some obscure way Janie's interest in George Landry quickened my own feeling and gave me emotions of vast superiority which were very bad for me. All this is brought vividly back to me by this page of Ellen's journal which recounts the final dénouement:—

> "We have been having an awful time this afternoon, and I don't think that any of us will feel the same ever again. Roberta has been crying in my arms and says she feels soiled, but she has acted so nobly that it will be a comfort to her, because being noble is always a comfort to Roberta—and to almost anybody else. George Landry has been a friend of Roberta's for some time, and when the other girls have joked her about it she has been very stern, and I've believed everything Roberta has said because I think it is horrid to do anything else. But Janie has been talking about George, too, in the way she goes on about anybody that notices her, only who could tell that Janie would talk about those who don't notice her in the least? This afternoon we were all talking together, and she began: 'Last night George Landry came past my house and I pretended not to notice him, and he stopped and said, "Can I come in?" And I said, "No, it was too late."' 'What time was it?' asked Mildred Dilloway. 'Oh, it was about eight o'clock, and he stayed and talked and talked and leaned clear over the gate, and I kept backing away, and if mother hadn't called me from the house,—' Here Mildred

broke in and said: 'Janie Acres! I don't see how you can tell things like that! George Landry was at my house all yesterday evening.' 'Well, it was the evening before that,' said Janie. 'Well, it wasn't the evening before that,' said Mildred, 'because he was at my house all the evening before, too.' 'I thought your mother was so particular,' began Janie; but Mildred wouldn't let her change the subject the way Janie knows how to do, and she said: 'The way you have gone on about George Landry has almost made trouble between George and myself. It has made me feel quite suspicious at times. But now I have caught you at it.' Janie blushed very hard and said: 'You are very spiteful, Mildred, about it. George Landry does like me and I haven't told you anything that wasn't so. Perhaps it wasn't so late when he leaned over my gate.' 'He wasn't anywhere near your old gate,' said Mildred, 'and I might just as well tell you—' And here Mildred, who is very soft when she loses her temper, and begins to cry, did all these and made us all very much embarrassed. 'And I might as well tell you—and you can see how much you have hurt me—he kissed me good-night. So you can see whether it's nice of you to pretend that George Landry is interested in you or not.' We were all perfectly quiet for a minute, and then it was that Roberta made her great sacrifice. Mildred was still crying from excitement and Janie was at a loss for something to say for once, and looking very frowning-browed and jealous. 'Girls,' Roberta said, 'I have something to tell you. And you, Mildred,—whether George has been attentive to Janie I don't know, but—' 'He walked home with me yesterday afternoon,' said Janie. 'He did not,' replied Roberta firmly; 'he did not. He was at my house all yesterday afternoon, and we were reading poetry and he held my hand.' If Roberta had been the least like Mildred, she would have cried, too, but she stood there straight and held her head up as beautiful as an avenging fate. What she said stopped Mildred's tears, and she sprang to her feet and stamped her foot, and said: 'Well, if he did that and then came to my house and did what he did in the evening, he's a pig!' And she stamped her foot again. 'I said the truth anyway'; and she glared at Janie who now said, 'I was just trying to tease both of you.' But Mildred snapped, 'You were trying to lie to both of us.' And Janie stuck her head on one side in the most provoking way and said, 'I don't want your horrid beau anyway.' It was all very painful, especially to Roberta. She said: 'We must never any of us speak to him again. He is unworthy of our notice. Except to spare you more pain, Mildred, I would not have told you about this at all, and I am very much ashamed of myself, and it serves me right. I shall never let any one hold my hand again as long as I live.' None of us knew that any boy could be so double-faced, and we all have agreed, and Janie Acres, too, that we shall act as though he did not exist at all, which will save our dignity and we hope will teach him something."

When other people write our lives, they tell the dates of our births, marriages, and deaths; they note the year we went to college and when we left, and all the other irrelevant things; no one says that it was at such and such a moment that his soul was born, or that the baptism of fire that turned away the selfishness of this woman came at such a time. We keep these great and obscure birthdays and many minor ones to ourselves, and this droll little episode was the definite ending for us of little-girlhood. In our town we dawdled along in what the Germans call the "back fish" age until some such thing has happened, for we had no custom of girls coming out all of a sudden full-blown young ladies; we had to win our spurs in a way.

We thought of ourselves as grown up, to be sure. Mildred Dilloway had had a very melodramatic love-affair with one of the lads in the seminary who had gotten into some sort of a scrape and was expelled from school. He had urged Mildred to fly with him. Alas! that women should be so practical. Even young as she was, she asked, "Where?" and when he had no special place to propose beyond his parents' house, to which he was then repairing, she had laughed at him, but in spite of all our experiments in sentiment we had remained immature in spirit. Now, suddenly, through the actions of this soft youth, George Landry, we found ourselves in an absurd position. The grown woman in us came to life; we wanted to vindicate ourselves in our own eyes; and it was during the next few months that we found ourselves suddenly grown up and the world's attitude toward us suddenly changed. From being the little girls who accepted the casual kindnesses of older men in a panic of gratitude, suddenly our position was of those who are sought out.

CHAPTER X

Ellen's formal renouncing of goodness helped us find our place in the grown-up world. Her gayety had always made her overstep the bounds of perfect decorum demanded of young women in my generation, and she set about carrying out her resolution which she told me about. I remember well the shocked sort of quiver with which I recognized myself, even staid Roberta, in her question:—

"Roberta, when you're in company, don't you ever want to do foolish things? When you see a lot of solemn people saying good-bye downstairs, don't you want to slide down the banister into their midst? When Edward Graham used to lecture me, again and again I've wanted to take his hand and skip down the street singing, 'Hippity Hop to the Barber Shop,' and see what he'd do. I've always wanted to do all the foolish things I've thought of when I was in company, and now, Roberta, I'm going to!"

I had had these erring impulses. Who has not? In each of us there is a hinterland where thoughts as fantastic as anything that happens in dreams gambol around with the irresponsibility of monkeys. Ellen translated a certain amount of these into action—and see what happened.

This is what makes virtue so discouraging in an imperfect world. It was her naughtiness which advertised to the world of men, "I am a sweet and adorable person; I can make you laugh, and I can make you dream, and I have no fear." Ellen now acted before strangers with the inspired foolishness which most of us keep for those best known to us. Even for them this mad spirit is not at our beck and call, but must wait for the time and place to bring it out. Youth, empty of such lovely, high-spirited, and drunken moments, must be very sad.

The divine folly of such mirth is only for the partaker; one must feel the wine of life coursing through one to understand its spiritual significance. Joy-drunken young people seem to outsiders silly, if they don't seem wanton; and while the things that we did would seem mild enough if I told them, they set our little New England town by the ears during the year that followed.

Our little coterie gradually acquired the reputation of giddiness among the older people, while we steadily became leaders among those of our own age, and Ellen the central flame around which we revolved. I myself thought her too audacious, and even when carried away by her I used to remonstrate seriously with her. This accomplished nothing, but it eased my own conscience.

Edward Graham, who had come back to teach in the academy, also lectured Ellen continually. He was one of those tenacious men who desire a thing all the more when they have lost it, and I think the full flowering of his affection for Ellen only came after he knew he couldn't have her. I think it might never have come otherwise. His love for her was deep and fundamental, and the sort of love men treat like the air they breathe; but had she married him and been the docile wife she would have been, he might never even have known himself to what extent he cared, and still less have shown it to her. They continued to see much of each other, because he had put to her the plausible story that they could still be friends, and she, of course, eagerly assented, wishing to make what little reparation she could, and not realizing that at the back of his mind was a determination to win her at whatever cost.

Now her growing popularity and light-mindedness caused him anguish. Her growing popularity aroused in him a leaden jealousy. He alternated from mad blame to pleading affection. His devotion to her was a continual pain, and yet in her gentleness she didn't know how to escape it, and his criticisms bred in her a certain defiance of the world and of conventions and made her more extravagant. I suppose it was because it came as a climax of a number of smaller follies that the town took so much notice of the famous "Young People's Party," given by the gentle Mr. Sylvester. I well remember the next day. I see myself demure in my grandmother's kitchen, demure and gingham-aproned, my hands in dough, my hair sleek under its net. I see Ellen, a blue ribbon around her hair, a sparkle in her eye, her little feet crossed, with all the look of the cat which has swallowed the canary, and is glad of it. This is what sin had brought her to, you see. Mrs. Payne sat, sweet and helpless-looking, in one chair, and my grandmother creaked portentously back and forth, her hands folded on the place she called her waist-line, saying to Sarah Grant:—

"It couldn't have been hens, Sarah."

"It was hens," said Miss Sarah accusingly. "They went out to the hen-yard and brought each hen into the house, and they flew around and broke two vases." Her eyes meantime had not quitted Ellen, who at this inopportune moment snickered with happy recollection. "Ellen," her aunt broke off accusingly, "did you think of bringing those hens into the house?"

"We were hawking," explained Ellen. "I brought mine in on my wrist and it flew across and perched on John Seymore's shoulder. That's how we told off partners for 'Authors'; everybody got a hen, and on whichever boy's shoulder it perched,—and often it wouldn't perch,—that's what really happened." She laughed; her mother laughed; I laughed.

Whoever reads this will sympathize with Aunt Sarah, because it doesn't seem witty for a grown company of young men and young girls to have behaved that way in the house of their minister. It had been a golden moment, I assure you,—a party that stood out;—and if ever the laughter of the Greeks was heard in that staid, old New England town it was when Ellen Payne stood aloft on the hassock, a squawking hen trembling indignantly on her wrist; and she at that moment looked both beautiful and absurd. Miss Sarah Grant saw nothing of all this.

"I am chagrined," she said. "Have you no respect for life?" And she walked away heavily.

Ellen spent the afternoon gathering expiatory pond-lilies of which her aunt was as a rule fond. She waded in the pond during the whole afternoon, her skirts trussed up scandalously, emerging with a stocking of black mud on either foot. She was sunburned, she was mosquito-bitten, she was happy, she sung aloud for joy on her way home; and when she left the offering at her aunt's door, this lady said: "These are very pretty, Ellen, and I thank you, but I wish, my dear, that you had made me some little gift that is a testimony of your industry."

It was on our way home that we were stopped by some women from the other church, who asked me:—

"Roberta, is it really true that you and Ellen started to bring in hens to the minister's house at the Young People's Party?"

"Roberta never started it," said Ellen, who was easily drawn in ways like this.

"We thought they were joking when they told us," said Mrs. Mary Snow, who was a widow and very precise.

"Well," said Miss Amelia Barton, "I should think Mr. Sylvester would have prevented it."

"Mr. Sylvester enjoyed it, the fowls enhanced the party," said Ellen. I pulled her along. "Hateful gossips," she said. As we passed the house where Edward Graham was living, this illustrious young man joined us for the purpose of saying:—

"You remember, Ellen, I told you at the party, when I first saw you coming in with the hen, that you had far better leave it outside. The whole town is talking and buzzing."

"The whole town disgusts me deeply," cried Ellen, "and so does any one who lets the buzzing reach my ears."

"You ought to want to know the reaction of the things you do," retorted Graham, whose belief in his moralities made him irritable when attacked. "You are criticizing Mr. Sylvester for permitting it and I think you went much too far."

When Edward Graham moralized on the subject Ellen replied flippantly:—

"It is that you and everybody else criticize anything you're not used to. What's the harm in hens; what evil does bringing a hen into the minister's house lead to? Does it make you want to go and take the amber beads off a baby's neck just because I brought in a hen and it perched on John Seymore's shoulder? John Seymore didn't mind it, and he's studying for the ministry. It is people like you, who talk about an innocent thing like a hen, and fuss over it as if it was something bad, who do harm," cried Ellen; and she swept me along with her. She comments in this fashion about the episode:—

"At the party we were all very happy, and there's no
rule that says that a thing must be of a worthy sort before
we may laugh at it. That's one of the nice things about

laughing, there's no rhyme or reason to it. It was not among those things that mother talks of that undermine our fineness of perception. But Mr. Sylvester didn't realize how people were going to feel about it, and now they are all talking and tongue-wagging as though something terrible had happened. Am I wrong, or are they? I think they are, and I hate them for it, and I feel as though that was the worst thing I had done, because I hate poor Edward Graham and I hate Mrs. Snow and Miss Barton because of their smallness and injustice; and aren't they more wicked to talk about innocent things and gossip about young people and make those who are happy feel uncomfortable and sinful? It makes me want to break a window when I think how virtuous they feel."

We hadn't heard the last of the talk concerning the "Hen Party." Rumors of it reached our ears from all sides. I suppose our elders exaggerated the talk, that we might learn decorum. Personally I could not imagine, any more than Ellen could, just what harm the hens had been supposed to have done us. One of the hardest things for me now to understand is the annoyance so many people feel at the sweet, noisy fun of young people. It seems to me the very laughter of fairyland, but older people have a way of turning the fairy coach of mirth into a pumpkin drawn by mice, and are proud of themselves for doing this.

It is strange that the ages of men have rolled on one after the other without this being a basic principle laid down to all parents — you can't disapprove a child into the paths of virtue any more than you can scold a man into loving his wife.

There are a great many young people who are made reckless and sullen by such disapproval, though Ellen was saved from the harm that Edward Graham and the public opinion of which he was the voice might have done her by the utter sympathy of her little mother. She joined in all our little gayeties; she laughed with us. So did Mr. Sylvester. He attended the next two or three young people's parties, explaining to Ellen with his gentleness: "They say, my dear, that I'm not a fit guide for youth, so I am going to try and learn to be so by being more with you."

Of course, for their pains, these two grown-up children of God were called overindulgent; it was prophesied that they would spoil us; yet it was this that kept Ellen's audacities always sweet.

However, even so, Ellen's future destiny was despaired of by Edward Graham.

"Ellen is in danger of becoming a jilt," he told me.

"She can't help it if people like her," said I; for I, myself, had changed a great deal from that rigorous opinion that one should be proposed to only by the man one intends to marry.

"Ellen has altered very much in the three years I have known her," said Edward.

"She has grown up," said I.

"She has not grown up in the way I hoped to see her."

"Then, why don't you turn away your eyes from the offensive spectacle?" I asked him cruelly, not knowing that this—poor fellow—was just what he couldn't do. But even I was inclined to agree with Edward Graham.

CHAPTER XI

The old Scudder place in those days was full of laughter and young people. We were happier there than any place else, and I have never known any parties gayer than those, where the only refreshments were weak lemonade and occasionally a batch of cookies. I remember once or twice on great occasions Miss Sarah Grant provided "refreshments."

There came a time when I agreed with Edward Graham that Ellen was going too far. This night I remember we were playing hide-and-seek all through the house—and you may be sure it was only in little Mrs. Payne's house that such a thing would be allowed; for, oh! how sacred the guest-room in my day and how solemn and suggestive of a funeral the parlors in all the rigor of their horsehair. The Scudder house was a magnificent place for hide-and-seek,—the ell connected with the front of the house by what was known in my day as a "scoot hole,"—sort of a half-sized door,—and more doors opened from downstairs to the outside air than any house I have ever seen. I was hiding in one of the rooms when I heard the sound of running, and Ellen dashed in, John Seymore in hot pursuit, Ellen's laughter trailing out gay-hearted, careless, and irresistible.

"Now, I've got you," cried John Seymore's voice; and to my horror and scandal, he kissed her and Ellen merely laughed, laughed as she might have had she been ten instead of twenty, having run away breathless from a kiss that she expected to get in the end, and over which she was only making a mock panic. It was a romping sort of a performance, because Ellen had slipped away from him without any sentiment, but I was shocked and pained— and, besides, I liked John Seymore and he liked me, and I didn't think such levity was becoming in one who was to become a minister. I sought Ellen out.

"I saw you," said I.

"I heard you under the bed," said Ellen.

"That's why you went out?"

"I didn't want to embarrass you," said she, grinning a naughty little-girl grin at me.

"You ought to be ashamed," I admonished.

"Do I look it?" asked Ellen.

Suddenly there rushed over me most poignantly the memory of all our immature aspirations for the uplifting of those we knew. In a great wave of sadness I felt that we were wasting our lives—and the boy that liked me most of all had kissed Ellen in a romp. Twelve o'clock had struck for me. I was little Cinderella.

I suppose I must have shown Ellen all I felt, for she had seen the new look in my eyes and all her impishness vanished, and she cried out: "Oh, Roberta dear!"—when we both heard voices shouting:—

"It's Alec! It's Alec Yorke!" And in strolled a grown-up youth with wide shoulders, and a fine, open-air, swinging way with him, and on top of it was perched the head of Alec Yorke, only Alec made over with that incredible change that comes between fifteen and eighteen years. He was a man grown, but from this face, so masculine in its youthful quality, looked the touching young eyes of Alec, blue and sweet, and fearless, angry blue. He was seized with a dumb shyness and shook Ellen's hand over and over again, while his eyes rested on her as if the sight of her fed the soul of him. After a while they drifted off together. Ellen wrote about this meeting:—

"I can't tell how strange this meeting with Alec has been. It was as though my dearest friend had been changed over and I had to find my Alec in this new grown-up boy, who was the same and so different; even his voice was different. And then all at once he began to tell me how much he cared for me, and I feel so ashamed. I feel ashamed just because he says that the memory of what I am like has kept him from doing things that he shouldn't; he said I've always seemed to him like a white light burning in his life. I seemed to myself so very silly. I have never had any one talk to me as he did. Every one else who has cared for me has wanted something for themselves and he wanted nothing. I know now that I've never cared for any one in my life, for the way I care means nothing compared to the way he cares for me. What little bit of love I had for Edward was nothing. I feel ashamed because I know so little beside this boy who is so sweet and knows so much. He doesn't even expect I shall care for him. He only wants to make me proud that he should have ever cared for me, and to be something just for that. The things he said were all very young and very quixotic, perhaps, but how much more beautiful than the things that older spirits think of saying, and if I ever care for any one, I pray to God that I shall only think of what I can give. We sat there for a long time, and he held my hand in his and told me again and again about myself, and it was as if I had seen a reflection of the me that I might be and that I ought to be in the dear things he said; and when I said: 'Oh, Alec, you don't know me; you have forgotten me,' he said, 'I look at you, Ellen; you're sweeter than you were, sweeter than even I remember you.' But everything he said he said in just a few words that were hard for him to say, but each little, difficult sentence had his true self in it, as though he had distilled his soul for me, and I am so light-minded and have been so careless and I have tried so little, but if any one can feel about me as Alec does, I can try, even though I can't care for him, to be a little bit more the person he thinks I am. I have found the only reason I've ever yet found for acting the way people want you to act, and that is to please the ones you love. Some of the foolish things you do may hurt some one you really care for. Roberta was shocked because John Seymore kissed me; but I know we were just romping, and at most, perhaps, I was a little bold. It is funny that just a little boy should open my heart so. Mother and Mr. Sylvester love the me I am, or rather a younger me—the naughty little girl whose naughtiness they know don't make much difference; but somehow he has seen the sweetest person I ever am. I feel I have been a long way off from her, just being trivial and playing the same game over again and not going on. I haven't felt before for very long that Life was a glorious battle, and that every day, and all one's days, one must fight an obscure and ever-encroaching enemy. I've got to go back to the mountain. I have been seeing things close to and putting the emphasis on little things. I wish I could write a letter to everyone I am fond of. I think it would go like this: 'Dear People: I am going to make you a present of all the small things I do that you don't like. It will be the things I do, not the way I feel, but when I feel so happy that I want to run down Main Street, I won't run any more. I don't think these little things matter, but as I haven't many things to give, I give you my foolish impulses.'"

I can't say that I remember any marked change of action in Ellen because of her change of heart, and I still had that rather breathless feeling when I perceived that she was what she called "happy in her feet," by which she meant that then it was she was so happy that she must go romping through our staid, little town, a graceful harlequin.

It was just now, however, that she learned something about Miss Sarah Grant that touched her and made her wish to put her newborn feelings toward life into immediate action. Miss Grant, who had always lectured us severely, it now seemed had defended Ellen against all comments.

"I enjoy the child's high spirits," we found her to have said. "This town should not expect conventional actions from the Grants in inessentials."

Finding this out, Ellen said to me:—

"She wants a sign of my industry; I'm going to buy her something beautiful."

"What with?" I asked, because actual money was scarce in the Payne household, and their tiny income was eked out by trading eggs and other things at the store; for in a day when most people raised everything themselves it was desperately hard for two ladies to make actual money.

"Well," considered Ellen, "Mrs. Salesby has gone away."

Mrs. Salesby was a gentlewoman who copied Mr. Sylvester's sermons, his handwriting being quite illegible. The sum paid for this work was trifling, the work demanded, long and laborious, and Ellen's handwriting I might call temperamental. Mr. Sylvester was at this time having a book of his sermons, which he called "Thoughts on Life," copied. So for long hours Ellen shut herself in Mr. Sylvester's dust-covered study and copied the inspired wanderings of his spirit which was what his sermons really were.

Living in such intimacy with his thoughts had a further effect on her mind. They were the musings of a mystic who was not too acquainted with the infantile tongue which mysticism must perforce employ since it forever and ever has tried to impress the emotions for which the spoken language has not yet coined exact phrases. Something of his inner meaning came to Ellen. She worked on with a serene joy.

At this time also Edward Graham ceased to be a disturbing presence in her life; for feeling the need of showing Alec the sort of a girl she was she told him her whole little story and he had applied to it the youth's rule-of-thumb logic and saw the thing as it really was. He gave Ellen the first sensible talk she had ever had on her relations with men.

As for Ellen's calm acceptance of Alec's devotion, she used the sophistries with which women from all time have accepted the sweet, undimmed love of those whom they consider boys. "He would, of course," —writes the candid Ellen,—"have cared for some one anyway at this time, and it is better that he should care for me because I place real value on his affection and try myself to be good so that I shall never hurt them."

Through months of toil she had at last acquired the few dollars necessary to buy the present, and something "boughten" at that moment had a tremendous value. Gifts were much fewer, and such gifts as there were were of course made at home.

The first afternoon after her long task was over, Ellen went up the mountain to reflect. Our mountain and our river were two things which moulded the souls of us. The austere mountain drew my eyes toward God, and how often I lost my personal grievances as I mingled my bemused little spirit in the swirling river, which, after one looked at it long enough and steadily enough, seemed at last to absorb one in itself and float one down seaward. I knew that Ellen was on the mountain and Alec and I walked up to meet her. She was on what we call "Oscar's Leap," a place where the mountain seemed cleft away above the river, as though with some giant's knife, and just above there was a clear platform, surrounded by trees and bushes. Our tradition had it that Oscar, one of the chiefs, leaped his horse into the river below to escape from his enemies.

This night the river was turned to a mighty sheet of burnished crimson, as the sun set just beyond the black bulk of the mountain. Our peaceful town took on an apocalyptical aspect. One felt that among the serene silence of departing day, the end of the world had come, and in some way the very silence of its coming made it more awesome, for its color demanded cataclysmal sounds. Ellen said once: "It tears one through like the noise of trumpets."

Presently Ellen came down the road toward us, the last slanting rays of the sun outlining her in the light. She didn't see us as she came toward us, as we stood in the shadow. As I look back at that time it seems to me that she forever moved in a pool of light that came from the radiance of her own spirit. There was a little hush over both Alec and myself.

He said: "She is very lovely."

And I answered: "She has been on the mountain."

I felt, indeed, as if Ellen had gone there to commune with God.

"When I came from the mountain to-day," she writes, "the world had a new look, as if I had never seen it before. I wish the river had a face so I could kiss it. I had to hold my hands tight so that I shouldn't fling them around the necks of Alec and Roberta; I took it for a good omen that the two that I love most should be waiting there for me. I have made a wonderful friend. Though I have never seen him before, yet I have known him always. I was sitting above Oscar's Leap, thinking hard, meditating on the beautiful things in life, which if you think hard enough about, Mr. Sylvester says, you will become like, but to do this you must feel like a little child, very small and humble and believing. I think I was nearer feeling this than I have since I was really little, when I looked up and saw him standing there. I had been thinking so hard I hadn't heard him come even; he was just there as if I had thought him into life, and I was no more afraid of him than as though I had always known him, although a stranger frightens me as a rule, unless I'm feeling foolish. He said: 'I have been watching you a long time; I've been watching you think'; and I just smiled at him and he sat down there beside me, and then it was as if all the things I had never been able to say to any one came to me, crowding to my lips. I don't know if I said them or not, because I don't remember exactly what we talked about. We made friends the way children make friends. I felt that if I knew him a little more only, he would know me more as I am than any one in the world, because the me, that my own people know, is so mixed up with that gone-forever person that used to be myself. I wish I could remember more what we said to each other, but the meaning of them is like Mr. Sylvester's sermons—we haven't got words for them yet; but I remember one thing that seems to me like the truth of truths. He said to me, 'Ellen, I am coming back to find you; it was more than chance that led me here this afternoon.'"

In all that she writes about him during the next two weeks, where he crosses and recrosses the pages of her journal continually,—for she wrote an almost day-to-day account, Time at that moment held its breath and gave her space to look at the treasure that had fallen into her hands,—she never once mentions the word "love." She merely waited for the coming of her friend. During this time little bits of their conversation creep out. They had told each other exactly nothing about their lives, drowned as they had been in the poignancy of their encounter.

I thought in my innocence that the white radiance of her, that was so apparent to me who loved her so, was the blossoming of religion in her spirit. One afternoon we had been notified that

Ellen's gift had come for her aunt. It had been sent direct from the city, very beautiful toilet and cologne bottles, I remember it was, of the massive kind with which ladies' dressers were then always supplied. We had it all planned that we were to sit there while Miss Sarah undid her parcel, and finally, after she had wondered who could have sent her this gift, with a gesture Ellen was to tell her, but while Miss Sarah was about to open the parcel, the wide door of the stately drawing-room opened. A young man was framed in it. He stood there looking at Ellen, who was sitting on a low hassock; she looked at him. It seemed to me that a breathless silence elapsed before Miss Sarah looked up, while these two talked mutely. I have only one other time in my life seen a look on any human face that was like hers. It was that of one who in another minute must hide her face in her hands to screen her eyes from the sight of the glory of the Lord.

CHAPTER XII

Thus they stood through an eternity of understanding, which in the actual flight of time was only the moment that it took for Miss Sarah to turn around, but it seemed to me that her glad little cry of surprise: "Why, it must be Roger!" was echoed deep in Ellen's heart; and turning to Ellen she said:—

"This is Mr. Roger Byington. You remember, Ellen dear, I told you he was going to stay with us.—But what a surprise—we didn't expect you until this afternoon."

"I started a day earlier so that I could walk over the mountain. I walked the last stage." He looked at Ellen, whose eyes had never once left him and who had the look of having seen a miracle. So poignant seemed her look to me, so much did it tell me, that I remember I had the wish to stand between her and this strange young man, so that her heart shouldn't be revealed to him, and between her and her Aunt Sarah, so that she would notice nothing; but I might have spared myself the pains. In a moment Aunt Sarah was leading him away to seek for Mr. Ephraim Grant.

I knew without Ellen telling me that this must be her friend of the mountain. She had told me about him in all naïveté. It had seemed to me sort of an Ellenesque thing to have happened, charming and delightful, though I had paid no attention to her belief that he was coming back.

"Did you know Mr. Byington was the one, Ellen?" I asked.

She shook her head. "How could I guess?"

We had been told that old friends of Miss Sarah's had written asking for a boarding-place for their son, who was reading law after his return from abroad and wished a quiet place where he might study, and that Miss Sarah had invited him to stay at her house, but naturally I had not connected him with Ellen's stranger.

Once in a long time things turn out the way that we dream that they will. Once, perhaps, in a lifetime all the dreamed-of and expected things focus themselves into one full moment. At such times the doors of our spirits open and we find the hidden roads to the spirits of others, and this was what happened to Ellen. Instead of Roger's arrival dimming her present, everything came about as she had planned and it all worked in together into one marvelous day. For once Age understood Youth, for when Miss Sarah learned how this money had been laboriously come by, she said:—

"Ellen, you have the heart of a child, for only a child would have treasured up my word that I meant and didn't mean, and I think, my dear, I've often scolded you for this very reason. You are a darling child, Ellen, but a trying one, and I hope you'll never grow up."

When Roger came back with Mr. Grant, "Look, young man," she said. "Do you know what this is? This is one of the rarest things in the world; it's a true gift. You have probably never made one in your whole life; you and your family go in and plank down your money and buy something pretty and go away. Now, whenever I look at this, Ellen, I shall think of your patience and self-denial,— yes, and your industry, and oh, dear, dear! I shall never be able to scold you again, which, as I know, you will often deserve."

We sat there for a half-hour and I felt as though I were in the midst of a story, with my Ellen for the heroine.

Roger won us all that afternoon. In conversation he was the most delightful person in the world. There was about him a certain, subdued arrogance when he wasn't talking, which changed when he smiled into the most delightful sunny winsomeness. He listened to those much older and those much younger than himself with an absorbed interest that gave the speaker the sensation of saying something of deep interest. Later we learned that this young prince and a trying bad little boy were the same person, but that day we only saw the young prince. I know that I myself had the impression of having had the window of Life suddenly thrown open wide, for with unconsciousness of what he was doing, he took us sweeping up and down the world. He had traveled a great deal in a day when traveling was much more of an adventure, and he had had adventures and real ones, as one of his temperament would be bound to have. He made one feel that one was living with a higher vitality, as Ellen did, and the way Ellen affected me then and later was as though she were a beautiful jewel that I had seen in the sun for the first time. On this first day she sat there shining with soft radiance and saying almost nothing, becoming, it seemed to me, transfigured before my eyes.

After a while Ellen rose to go, and Roger accompanied us, and I had to stay with them, having no pretext for leaving, as my house was beyond Ellen's down the street; but it seemed to me that, without meaning to, they subtly shut me out by the very way that they included me in their laborious conversation, for as soon as we three were walking down the sidewalk, under the great double row of elms which bordered our street, their touching courtesy made a stranger of me as nothing else could have done. Ellen wrote:—

"The first thing he said to me when we were alone was, 'Ellen, I thought you were a little girl and you're grown up. When you meet strange men on the mountains and they say to you politely, "May I ask your name?" do you answer, "Why, I am Ellen"?' I had forgotten that I had said that. I suppose I did look young, with my hair down and my brown dress that's so much too short for me. 'I came back to find a wonderful little girl; where is she?' I answered,—and my heart was beating at my boldness,— 'She grew up while you were away.' 'Oh, Ellen, Ellen!' he said to me, 'those were the longest weeks in all the life I've lived, and it's strange it should have been your aunt's house that I should have come to. It is as if I had been led by the hand, first, to you on the mountain, and now, to you here.' And then he looked at me and said, 'Ellen, you focused all my life for me that day on the mountain. I've spent two weeks clearing from my life worthless trash, all the débris that a man accumulates living as many years in the world as I have.' And he has really lived in the world, ever since boys here are nothing but boys. He told me, 'When I went by I stopped at our place on the mountain. Have you been back?' 'Yes,' I said, and I looked down. 'Look at me,' he said, and it seemed to me he drew my eyes to his. 'Have you been there often?' 'Yes.' 'How often, Ellen?' and I shook my head. I felt as though I was dying of shame, for I had been there every day at sunset. What if he knew how I had worked to get everything done so I could fly up there at sunset? I felt as if his eyes were burning down into my heart and he said, as though he could read my thoughts, 'Every sunset I remembered the way I saw you there. I ought to have seen you there again, Ellen; I wanted to take you and fly up there, and I am going to get a good mark in heaven for having been so nice to your aunt and uncle, and even to your nice little friend, for being so terribly in my way.' And all of a sudden he looked like a naughty, bad, little boy, which made me laugh at him, and made me feel on earth again;—and now I'm going to see him at sunset. I feel as if I had never been alive before. I went in and kissed mother and she said: 'Was your aunt pleased with the present, dear?' I had forgotten all about my aunt and all about the present. It was as though I had returned from a very far-off country."

CHAPTER XIII

That afternoon we were all quilting at our house and Miss Sarah was pleased enough to give an account of her guest.

"I've had a long letter from Lucia Byington," she said to my grandmother, "explaining that precious scapegrace of a son of hers, but I can tell Lucia she might have spared herself the pains. The minute I clapped my eyes on him I knew all about him, having known his father and mother. He has all her charm and her willfulness, with the iron will and talent of his father. I suppose, because I'm an old maid, I can't understand why a man can't bring up a high-metaled son, exactly like himself, without being at odds with him. But there! He expects his son to start where he's left off, with all the sobriety and solemnity of an aged Solomon. And why people like Lucia and David should expect not to have trouble with their children, I don't know. And as for David, he fights his own youth in the boy. Now the time had come for Master Roger to stop skylarking over the earth; he was holding out; leave town he wouldn't. They had words; he slung a knapsack on his back and went off, and wasn't heard from for a week, and then came back as meek as the Prodigal."

You may be sure that Ellen and I had our ears wide open to this story, knowing as we did why it was that Roger had suddenly become the docile son. We were so self-conscious that our eyes did not dare seek one another's, and we sewed together the large, gay squares of patchwork with the precision of little automatons.

My grandmother spoke up:—

"Well, Sarah, I half dislike having your stormy petrel in our little town. I saw him this morning, and he seemed to me a restless-looking bird. He'll be turning the silly heads of our girls next."

"Let me catch him at it, or them, for that matter!" cried Miss Sarah. "He's here for work, and not to worry me with such-like goings-on! You may be sure that his family have had trouble enough with him in such imbroglios already."

We had tea early and did the dishes and fell to our quilting again. I noticed Ellen becoming more and more abstracted until finally Miss Sarah said:—

"Well, Ellen, try to bring your mind back to your work. Years haven't taken your habit of 'wool-gathering' from you."

Ellen wrote about this:—

"When I was a little girl I was more afraid of the setting sun than anything in the world and now I know why, for I was waiting always for this moment to come, when the sun, red and round and menacing, set right before my eyes and I stared hopelessly and hopelessly into it, not able to move. I had that awful leaden feeling of wanting to move and not being able to, as though I had been quilting through the ages and listening to stories about Roger, a strange and distorted Roger, who was as infinitely far away from me as the sun, and yet that I must go to him. I knew he was there at Oscar's Leap, and I felt as if he called my soul out of my body and my body suffered. I tried to tell myself that there was to-morrow. I tried to tell myself how foolish I am to be so broken in two that I must needs go and keep my word with this man that I've seen only twice in my life; but though I have only seen him twice, I've known him always, as I said before. There's no friend as dear and close as he in all the world. Oh, beautiful day that I can never have! The things that we would have said to each other to-night, we will say them another time, but not in the same way. This day is lost to me and I can never have it back again."

She tells this of the time when next she saw him:—

"It seemed to me as though he leaped at me, there was such gladness in his face, although any one across the street would have said he just walked. He said, 'Oh, Ellen, Ellen!' as he did before; and then, 'I've been waiting ever since I saw you'; and then his face turned stern, and he said, 'Ellen, why didn't you come? Are you like other women; while I've been away did that candid, little girl learn to hide herself and learn to be false to her word?' I thought I should cry; tears came to my eyes; it seemed so cruel that at the very first I should fail him this way, and he saw how I felt and said to me, 'Oh! don't, don't, dear.' And for a little while we walked on in silence. 'Where were you, Ellen?' he asked me; and he stood still in the path and said: 'Ellen, are you a coward? What chained you there? Didn't you hear me calling to you from the mountain? Couldn't you get up and walk out of the room? If you had gone and hadn't come back, what would have happened?' And then he looked at me in a way I shall never forget, and what he said I shall remember all my days, for so I am going to live. 'Ellen,' he said, 'you and I in our friendship are not to be tied down by rules. Remember, courage opens all doors. Ellen, I threw away many things to clear the road that led to you. Let us keep on that way, Ellen; put your hand in mine and promise. We'll walk to each other straight out of the open door, without fear, won't we?' When I got home, I am so foolish and I am so weak and merit his friendship so little, that I cried. I don't now understand why it was that I stayed this afternoon."

In this brave and heady fashion Roger began his wooing of Ellen. Just as his whole pose, forward swinging head and relaxed body, gave one the impression of one ready to make a forward rush at any moment and seize what it wanted, so was the action of his spirit. It was like the wine of life to my Ellen. They saw the sunset on the mountain together every night that they could, and he came down the pasture that led down from the hill, through the meadow, to the brook back of the Paynes' house. About these things I knew, for Ellen needed a confidante. Love overflowed her, and this was no secret, little love which she carried shyly, a secret lamp by which to light her way, which she hid as soon as any one appeared; but this was a flaming thing, as hard to hide as a comet. It swept her up and out and beyond herself into that over-heaven that only the pure in heart can feel when they are in love.

It was only a very short time when she stopped deluding herself with any terms like "her dear friend"; for one of Roger's great strengths, then and always,—and I think to this day,—was knowing exactly what he wanted, and taking the shortest way to it, and to get his desire he was splendid and ruthless, and beware to any one who stood in his way.

It was about now that she began the habit of writing what she called "Never Sent Letters"; for could she have been with him all the hours of the day, the day would yet not have been long enough for her, and they saw one another what seemed to them only now and then. She writes to him at this time:—

"What did I do with my time before I met you? The days that I've spent before you came have no meaning now to me, and now that I am away from you the only preparation is for you. Everything that I see, everything that I think, all my thoughts, I save them up and give them to you, tiny flowers from the country of my heart. I wonder how it is that you can love me ever so little, who have so little to give to you who have so much, and the only bitterness that I know is that what I have to give you is so worthless. You say that you love the joy of life in me. I wish I could make all the joy I feel shine out like a flame. I wish that I could distill all the love I have for you into one cup and then give it to you that you could drink, for entirely and utterly I am yours and have been yours always and forever, and so shall always be until I am changed over into some one else. When I'm with you I don't dare tell you these things for fear that I should drown you in myself. Take my life and do what you like with it, for without you it is a thing valueless to me."

In this way was Ellen's touching prayer answered—that when she loved any one she wished only to give.

For the time being everything else was blotted out for her; she had this measureless, sky-wide joy of giving herself and all day long, and all the time her spirit went out toward him in incense. Her days were lost in contemplation of the wonder which had happened.

"From the moment I leave him, I walk toward him," she wrote—and in the interim between she went on apparently with life as before, and this woke in her a still wonder.

> "It is so very strange to be doing the same things that I was before, but all the work I do for my mother, every book I read, every word I speak has a meaning that it hadn't. It is as though my ear were at the heart of Life and I heard Life beat."

CHAPTER XIV

I saw a good deal of her and so did Alec. Alec at this time was preparing to work his way through college. Even Roger, who treated the village youth with the kindly tolerance of a splendid young prince, treated Alec as an equal. Alec, of course, gave him the whole-hearted admiration that generous lad does a man.

He guessed Alec's infatuation for Ellen, for Roger was one of those experienced gentlemen who feel far off any emotional flurry and he had paired all of us before he had been in town ten days, and that without having appeared to observe us. So much was he the over-masculine that nothing of this kind could come near him without his senses registering it. He could mention John Seymore's name in a way to make me blush and make me wish to stamp my foot on the ground with outraged modesty. And as for Edward Graham, it was on his account that Ellen first learned the terrible anguish that love may bring with it, and she wrote:—

"I have learned how foolish I am and how weak. We were both at Oscar's Leap looking down into the river. 'I walked up and down the earth, Ellen,' he said, 'looking for you, and as I looked from one person to another I said, "No, that's not Ellen," and then I didn't know your name. I feel that it's strange of me that I should not have guessed it.' 'Didn't you ever care,' I asked him, 'for any one for a moment?' 'No,' he said, 'how could I? Once in a while I saw some one that looked a little like you and there I waited longer.' 'But people must have cared for you,' I said. 'Not really; some people make a game of things like that, Ellen,' he said. And already I felt deeply ashamed, that though I am so much younger I should have been so foolish as to think I cared once. 'And you, Ellen; you waited the same way for me, didn't you? The people who cared for you, you knew weren't me.'—And then I told him about Edward. He didn't speak for a long time, and then he said: 'Isn't there anywhere on the earth a woman so young and so sheltered that she doesn't pass from one hand to another and snatch at love, and give a piece of herself here and a piece of herself there? But, Ellen, I thought you were different'; and the deep and bitter shame that rushed over me then I don't think I shall ever forget. He asked me a great many questions, and when he found that I was so little when it all happened he forgave me. It seems wonderful to me that he should have waited."

It seems wonderful to me, as I read this little, pitiful account, that Ellen with her straight, clear mind should have let herself be so bemused as to feel that something was wrong which her own inner sense had told her was not wrong, honest as she had always been with herself. She lived for the first time by another person's standard for her. She had given him that most precious thing of all, her inner judgment of herself. It seems still more wonderful to me that Roger should have told her such a story, for he had had love-affairs a-plenty; but I think he was utterly honest in this, and in his honesty lay his danger and his charm. New emotions, as they came to him, came with so overwhelming a force that they wiped out not only the old love, but the memory of it, and when he had fallen in love with the wild sweetness of Ellen the other experiences in his life seemed to him only an unimportant outburst of passion. Yet for her he had the Turk's jealousy: he wished not only for the utter virginity of the body, but also for the virginity of the spirit to such a point that he had to make-believe that there had been no Edward in her life at all before he could "forgive."

They had both imagined that they could keep their love a secret for a while until Roger should have done a certain amount of work.

"I want my parents to love the idea of Ellen from the first," he told me, "and I've been so at cross-purposes with them that I want to get back into their good graces a little before I tell them." And, indeed, for Roger to have rushed away to a tardy acquiescence of his father's will and to reappear immediately with a bride, we understood would strain the patience of an irascible parent. Just how much we learned from Miss Sarah, whom we heard saying:—

"The boy really seems to have turned over a definite new leaf. Lucia writes that she has learned that Roger has not even once written to that woman, whose entanglement with Roger worried them all so. She's been ill ever since he left, and it serves her right, too. A married woman of her age should have had better sense than to have let herself be carried away by an attractive youngster. Young rascal!—to go off on such a tangent when he was apparently just on the brink of making an ideal marriage. He and Emmeline Glover, you know, had been sweethearts for a long time when he got into this scrape."

In such a way were Ellen and I enabled to piece out Roger's life, and it apparently did not occur to her to make any comparison between herself and Roger; for in very truth the desire he had for her had swept from him all his former life until it seemed so paltry and meaningless that it was no desire of concealment that had led him to speak so lightly of both of these women. They had walked across his conversation with Ellen. Ellen had heard Roger's side of these stories.

"This married woman of whom they speak," she explained to me, "was a good friend of his and very much older than himself, but people are so evil-minded in this world. As for Emmeline Glover, he called her a sweet, little, silver-gray cloud, and another time, a graceful shadow."

We realized, however, that some time should elapse before Roger should tell his parents of his new love, or they would think it a weak passing interest and fail to treat it seriously.

When his interest in a person flagged, he lacked the coxcombry that makes a man afraid that his lack of interest has broken a woman's heart. Quite the contrary, he was apt to despise them for having shown affection for so light a cause. In the world of the affections he related nothing that had happened to him before to anything which was happening; each experience was fresh to him, a rising tide that had no memory of any other tide before.

They might have gone on with their indiscreet friendship indefinitely, but they counted without themselves. They were caught up, both of them, in the fierce moving stream that sweeps and swings people out of the orbit that they have planned. It was impossible to both their natures, under the stress of what they were feeling, to wish to be guarded. The clandestine element in their friendship, slight though it was,—for Ellen's little mother was taken into the secret, how could she leave her out; she needed to spill some of her happiness over on every one who came near her,— became very irksome.

Roger told me that he longed to go down Main Street shouting: "I love Ellen and am going to marry her; I love Ellen." And he would say with his naughty, little-boy look: "Whenever I hear Aunt Sarah"—for with what Miss Sarah called his usual impudence, Roger called her "Aunt Sarah" from the beginning—"talking about what a good boy I am and 'high time, too'"—and here he mimicked Miss Sarah's manner—"I want to say to her: 'Don't you know, you blind old fossil, that I'm here because of Ellen—Ellen—Ellen— Ellen, the gentle, that you presume to correct; Ellen, the joyful; Ellen, the glad of heart?' One of the strangest things in life to me is the impudence of Age, that dares to presume to touch so lovely a thing as Youth, and especially the youth of my Ellen. I can't stand it much longer, Roberta. Think of my knowing and submitting to my father's standing between Ellen and me. He's a wise old man, but he's forgotten things more useful than any that he knows, and I know them!"

And, indeed, he seemed the incarnation of the splendid and arrogant Knowledge of Youth, and my heart beat that so splendid a youth should be Ellen's; they seemed then God-appointed for each other.

Roger's direct mind found a way out of the difficulty. They were at their favorite meeting-place, up above Oscar's Leap, and looking out at the river which had turned to flame in the sunset light. Ellen tells about it:—

"'Oh, Ellen!' he said, 'why can't you put your hand in mine and walk out into the sunset with me? I often wonder why, when people love each other as we do, why they let anything stand in their way.' And then he said: 'Ellen, why shouldn't we—why shouldn't we walk out together, just you and me to-night?' And I said, 'Very well.' 'Come, then,' said he; and he held out his hand, and if I had put my hand in his he would have come with me, but I thought then he was joking. He said, 'Ellen, I'm not joking; I mean it. Would I joke of such a thing? Why should we waste one moment of what is so beautiful? You belong to me, Ellen, don't you?' And then he put his arms around me and kissed me so that I could hardly breathe, and said, 'Ellen, do you belong to me?' I could only hide my head on his shoulder and whisper to him, 'Yes'; and he said to me, 'Will you come with me, then, bad girl?' And I said, 'How can I?' 'Think about it, Ellen,' he said; 'think about it. I'll give you this week to think of it in, and at the end of the week it's one thing or the other. You come with me and be married or I'll tell them all. Am I one to tiptoe around through life, hiding because a cross-grained old man who happens to be my father will oppose at first something he will in the end be glad of?' He was such a bad little boy as he said this that I laughed, though he shouldn't speak of his father this way, I am sure, even though it is his father's fault. It is a terrible thing when any one as sweet and as full of the desire to love people as Roger shouldn't have been understood by his parents at home. His mother is very sweet, but she has never known how to get at him. All the mutinous things in Roger, and all the times when he wasn't adjusted to life, should have been loved away and understood away. He said to me: 'I've been good only since I have known you, Ellen, because no one has loved me before.' People have loved me all my life, and Roger, who is so much fuller and better than I, has not had my chance."

Here we have the tragedy that all mothers must face. Their sons, that they have brought up so tenderly and whom they have anguished over, bring all their mistakes to the beloved to be wept over. If you have worn a callous place in his spirit, the soft hand of his sweetheart will find it and she will grieve over it.

All girls are sure of two things: that they understand their men better than their very mothers do, and that they love them better as well; and every woman in the world, who is harrowing her soul over her little son that she is bringing up, may be sure that somewhere else in the world there is growing up a girl who is later on going to find any hardness or unkindness that she has left in his spirit. When she had known him six weeks, Ellen could have brought up Roger better than he had been. It was her first excuse for his willful idea. At first she didn't take him seriously, but opposition was the food on which his will fed. His father said of him that there was almost nothing one couldn't oppose him into. He thought out all the practical details. They could drive to the home of a minister he knew and be married at once and come back after two weeks.

"Oh! why," Ellen wailed,—"why should we make them all unhappy when all you have to do is to work a month or two more?"

"Yes, and then a long engagement, and then a making of my way; I in Boston, Ellen, and you here." It was a moment of terrible conflict for her. She wrote one of the letters to Roger she didn't mean to send:—

"Oh, my dear! I told you this afternoon and I want to tell you again in this letter how sweet this little hour is to me. It seems to be the sunniest place in all of life. The world seems to me to stretch ahead wonderful and splendid, and the great storms of Heaven whirling through the sky, and the lightning and the clouds, and I can hear in my ears the roar of cities and the big tumult of seas, and here it is so sweet. Why hurry away from it? Here it is so safe. The days of one's life when one is a girl and loves one's man are so few. Oh, don't hurry me away. Here is sunlight, and out there where you want to go it seems to me darkness. I'm a little girl, afraid of the setting sun. I was afraid of it and yet I couldn't help looking at it in its awful splendor. I couldn't take my eyes off from it, as little by little it dropped down behind the mountain, so wonderful and so inexorable. My heart chokes the same way when I think of running off in the night with you. Let's stay here with our hands in each other's and then quietly go out into life together without wrenching ourselves away from so many ties and without rending everything that links us to this life that we now live. Every bit of me, [she writes,] all my soul, all my heart and my mind, and all my body wants to go with him as he says, but oh! the needless hurt to them. When I said, 'Oh! how could we take our happiness at some one else's hurt?' he said, 'Listen, Ellen; the hurt is only temporary—just for a moment. Supposing we went to-morrow night and then we came back after two weeks married. My father, of course, will like you by and by—he just doesn't want any one for me now; he wants me to go on working and I am working like a giant, and then we would be free to go where we want.' Oh, it would be so easy! Nights I can't sleep, and when I do I am always deciding and deciding over and over again. When I tell him to remember the talk that it will mean, he says to me: 'Are you afraid?' I tell him, 'No, not for myself; but my mother will be left behind and there will be Mr. Sylvester and my aunt all to bear talk, so we shall be happy.'"

It seemed as if it was an unequal battle, all the forces of love, and Ellen's own nature even, waging a conflict with her little, soft heart. She grew pale under the strain. I noticed it, but I didn't know the cause, for here was something that naturally she didn't tell me, being allied with the forces of order as I was. She would have given him anything that she had to give, from her life on, but she could not bear to deal him out some one else's happiness with a careless hand. For his lack of understanding in this she writes:—

"He's never known what it is to have a home or people that you really love about you, or to be part of things."

He was clever in his arguments. Ellen writes:—

"He fairly argued my soul from my body. He said to me, 'Ellen, it is not as though they didn't want us to marry. It's just better for us to go together right away. Why should we waste a blessed year of our lives?' 'How could I run the risk of being the cause of serious trouble between you and your father and mother?' I said. 'You'll have to leave those things for me to judge,' he answered. 'How could I interfere with your work?' He grew almost angry at me. Then he threw his arms around me in that way he has, as though he would fairly crush my life from me, and he said: 'Ellen, Ellen, for my sake do it. I am not stable; I'm weak, and weak with violence. In you I found all the things that I haven't, all the sweet and all the true things in life, the things that I've been just for a minute at a time, when I've been a good little boy. You don't know me, Ellen. You've only seen the me that you made, but you can keep that if you want to. Don't play with it, Ellen. It's the most important thing in life for me to keep the me that you call out. I didn't know I could be so happy in a quiet place. I've always asked of life more and more, more life all the time and life has meant action, adventure, and danger, and all at once I find in you more life than anywhere else, and I don't want anything but you. Ellen, how can you continue this way to me for an idea, a foolish, bad idea, a taught idea? That's where you're not true, Ellen. If you were true, you would just put your hand in mine and walk away.' 'If there was no one in the world but you, I would put my hand in yours and do whatever you told me, but I'm not just I alone,' I told him. 'Well, I am just I, just I, and frankly in need of you—and in need of you right away. Ellen, this conflict with you is destroying me. By to-morrow night you must have decided.' I feel as though I had been shaken by a great wind. When I hear him crying to me, it seems as though he were crying for the safety of his soul; and yet there must be something hard in me, because I know that being without me for a few months more or less will not destroy a hard thing like Roger, and all the time my foolish and weak heart likes to pretend that it believes that this is so. But yet, how can I get the strength to tell him to-morrow night that I won't do what he wants me to? Oh! it is torture unspeakable to be ungenerous in any way to the one whom one loves. I can't do it. I've got to go, not because I believe down deep in me any argument that he has given me,—I was strong as those against it,—but just because he wants me to, because I can't help giving him whatever it is he asks."

Thus goes the age-old cry. She writes to him:—

"Oh! my dear, why will you make me make you such a sad gift? Oh! my dearly beloved, must I give to you the peace of mind, even for a little while, of all those whom I have loved in the world; and yet, I know myself that when I give you this that I shall be glad of it. Now that I have decided, my heart sings aloud. Somehow all that they will suffer seems small to me and unimportant beside this great, sweeping gladness that I feel.... I feel the way that you feel, nothing matters except that we should be together. Every day that we spend apart is a day wasted—but I can't think of the rest of it. It isn't so hard—it isn't so difficult, after all. We will come back and everything will be all right, although I feel when I say this as if it wasn't I, and that what carried me along was the black current of a river on which I was floating, and that I had been floating on it for always, only thinking before that I could direct my poor, little boat. Now I know that it is something quite outside myself that's swinging me on with the strength of this fast-rushing stream."

I remember that day very well. Ellen spent the day with me and with Alec, and we all three lay under the trees together and then Ellen went on a little tour of inspection. What she was doing really was saying "Good-bye" to the place that she knew and to us. Her eyes were bright and shining; I suppose she was thinking, "To-morrow I shall be where?—to-morrow I shall be who?—and these dear people who love me, what will they think? Not that I care!" She was so sweet to Alec that her loveliness melted his poor heart still further.

So sweet she was that, with one of those ironies of fate that are often more cruel than tragedy, Alec took this time to tell Ellen about the work he had decided to do. I can see him as he stood under the apple trees, the sun shining on his mane of hair, the brightness of his eager eyes contrasting with his self-consciousness, while we two girls stood there, each absorbed in her own affairs.

"I've looked all around life to see what I could do best—and I guess I know more about boys than anything else. I sort of know how they feel inside all the time. I don't forget. So I'm going to teach 'em. Try and teach 'em the things they want to know most and that they knock their shins so trying to find the way to. They have a hard time. I had just one teacher—and he led me out of darkness; and that's what I'm going to do. It's a business, you know, that means trying to understand all the time. It's a present to you, Ellen," he added with his crooked, whimsical smile.

He was so anxious that we should see what he meant, and we were so polite and innerly so blank. Teaching grubby little boys seemed to us an uninspiring profession for a splendid youth like Alec. We couldn't know how many years he had looked ahead. Alec and his gift to Ellen seem to typify man and woman. Man, who comes with his bright visions of the future, bestows the gift of his high dreams on girls who see nothing in them—and are polite. But Ellen was too heart-rendingly sweet that afternoon to seem anything but understanding. She was heart-breakingly gay.

After a while we went in together to Mrs. Payne's house. She and Mr. Sylvester were standing in the drawing-room with their hands clasped, and Mr. Sylvester spoke and said, "We may as well tell these dear children first"; and Ellen's little mother said, as shyly as a girl, "Mr. Sylvester and I have found very suddenly that we have always loved each other."

He rejoined with his deep simplicity of manner, "Yes, quite suddenly we found out that we've been to one another as the air we breathe, and as the water we drink, and as the sun that shines."

"And so, of course," said the little mother of Ellen, "we will be married."

She stood there violet-eyed, in her neat, little black dress, as slender as a girl, more girlish in her looks than many of us for all her forty years. I don't think that any of the three of us had realized that people as old as Mr. Sylvester and Mrs. Payne could live in the land of romance and could fall in love. Like most young people in their early twenties, we imagined that this great gift of mankind was for us alone and that it never lightened up the hearts of those who had already lived and loved; but as these two stood, hand in hand, there rushed over all of us the feeling that they were just great children. The look of wonder was in their eyes; they had been living for so long close to the land of enchantment, and just now had stepped over its borders into its realization.

"We see no reason for delaying our marriage long. We waited long enough; we've been close friends for eight years; and you, little Ellen,"—he spoke as though speaking to a little child,—"you have been already like a daughter to me and like a little mother to my children."

"You'll help me now, Ellen, won't you?" pleaded her little mother; and it was as though they had changed places and Ellen were the older. But Ellen had them folded in her arms, kissing first one and then the other, and we all followed suit; and for once the stern conventions of New England reserve, which held in its iron grip such sweet and simple spirits as Mrs. Payne and Mr. Sylvester, was broken through.

Now Ellen had a shining face, now everything had all been settled for her by Life. She could not possibly go away and leave her mother at such a moment, nor, of course, would Roger ask her this, and for a moment the light that swept over the country of her heart was dimmed by the quiet radiance of these two middle-aged people. Glad-footed she started off to her trysting-place, and what happened there was as though the sun had been eclipsed in mid-heaven, as though the solid earth had shaken under her feet. She ran to Roger with this precious tale of her mother's happiness in her hands, sure that he would understand. She writes, almost with an unbelief in the fact that she had herself heard and witnessed:—

"He wanted me to go with him just the same! He came forward to me in that way that always makes me think of leaping flame and said: 'You've decided to go, haven't you, Ellen?' And when I told him, he said, 'That makes it simpler, doesn't it? They'll be so occupied with themselves that they won't care what you do. Hooray!' And he laughed like a little boy. I said, 'You don't understand; now I can't go; I can't darken her happiness; my mother needs me'; and he stood before me, looking at me with eyes that burned with anger of his desire. 'Ellen,' he said, 'decide now, the long engagement with its perils for you and for me; my good or their good; our happiness against a few stitches put in your mother's clothes.' I said, 'I can't go.' He drew me to him and said, 'Ellen, are you coming? You must come'; and I felt as if my soul was shuddering out of my body, as if he tore me in two, and part of me must go, and I don't know what there was in my soul stronger than myself, because all of me never wanted to do anything more than to do his will, which was my will, too; but I had to say, 'I can't do it.' I know now that there are a thousand things that make up this; Mr. Sylvester being a minister, it would hurt him to have his daughter—oh! what a sweet word—run away. All these things, all the tangled and manifold ways in which my life is woven into those beloved of me, and now a thousandfold more tightly woven than before into the life of this little place, all held me back where the inner, beating heart of me cried aloud to go. He stood there pleading, and he raged with anger;

his words beat me down, shivering, like a heavy storm of wind and rain. The love of him drew me toward him, as flowers lift up their heads to the sun, but something deep down kept saying, 'No, I can't go. No, I can't go.' 'Now, I know,' said he, 'at last how little your love is worth'; and then he pulled me to him and kissed me roughly, and again and again, and then almost threw me from him. 'Good-bye, Ellen,' he said; and I cried, 'Where are you going?' 'Oh, not far,' he said; but I felt as if his spirit had gone to the end of the world, and he strode without me down the road. I am writing like one in a dream, because I can't see and don't know what's going to happen to us, and I want to run out into the night and run to his house and cry under his window that I'll go whenever he says, but then I know, if I did that, that at the last moment I would decide I couldn't go."

CHAPTER XVI

While Ellen was going through these hours of anguish her mother and Mr. Sylvester sat in my grandmother's kitchen, a pair of helpless, middle-aged children, discussing how they would break the news to Miss Sarah Grant. They didn't need to explain why Miss Grant would disapprove of their marriage; she would disapprove of it just as all the town would, for it was evident that if Mr. Sylvester was going to marry again it was his duty to himself and to his children to marry a "capable woman," and you might as well ask a moon-ray or a soft breeze in the trees to be capable as Ellen's little mother.

"I have suggested," said Mr. Sylvester, "that we let Miss Sarah learn of it as we shall the rest of the town. A simple and efficacious way has occurred to me, Mrs. Hathaway, of informing all our friends,—I shall merely tell Mrs. Snow and Miss Nellie Lee and then nature will do the rest." He was quite grave and simple-hearted as he said this, but I know that Alec and I did not dare to meet one another's eyes, for the good man had mentioned not only two of the most talkative ladies in town, but also two who had, according to gossip, felt themselves very capable of taking care of an incapable but godly man. Mrs. Payne, however, insisted that Mr. Sylvester should himself tell her sister of their engagement.

"My dear," said Mr. Sylvester, "I trust I am a soldier of the Lord, but I confess to a feebleness in the knees when it comes to confronting Miss Sarah, for both of us have been a serious anxiety to her even in an unmarried state, and what shall we be now when my housekeeper has gone?"

"And, indeed, my dear, how do you suppose," inquired my grandmother whose spiritual attitude had been one whose hands and eyes were both raised to Heaven,—"how do you suppose you are going to take care of the children?"

Ellen's little mother considered a moment.

"I shall love them," she replied after an interval.

Mind you, this statement was one of sheer anarchy in an age when discipline was the keynote with children and the superstition still flourished that one could not properly bring up a child without the rod.

"Yes," said my grandmother, "I suppose you will love the holes out of their clothes and love their gingham aprons into being, won't you?"

"I can depend upon Matilda a good deal," considered Mrs. Payne; "but we have scarcely had time, dear Mrs. Hathaway, to think of the material side of the question, and the children adore Ellen."

"And so, all together," rejoined Mr. Sylvester, "we shall get along very well, but our only real trouble is the pain of breaking the news to Miss Sarah."

"Well," said my grandmother, with brisk sarcasm, "if that's all that's troubling you, I'll tell her myself. I'll go to her and tell her that there's going to be a family consisting of two grown people, one grown girl, and three helpless little children, none of whom realizes that meals have to be got or housework done."

"Or, indeed," rejoined Mr. Sylvester, "where no one is occupied in anything but considering the lilies, how they grow."

Upon this the two smiled at each other, for they both had the wisdom of the simple in their spirits. However, it was apparent to any one what a helpless ménage this would be with the strong hand of Mrs. Gillig, the housekeeper, removed from it.

The news of the marriage ran through the town the way fire spreads; from house to house it galloped, then it would seem to skip a space and then mysteriously break forth afresh, as though by spontaneous combustion, and their interested chatter hid Ellen from herself a little. She wrote:—

"All day I have been receiving calls and answering questions. A certain sort of vague envy has mingled itself with a more definite commiseration and there has been a great deal of affection mingled with everything. They don't know. They all talk as though my little mother were a baby, and so she is. She's a child of light. She has not grown up and she hasn't made me grow up, and I hope I shall never have to, and I want to say to all the people,

'Oh, you blind person, you blind person,' when they speak in this half-patronizing tone of her. I want to say: 'Don't you know how much more she has than you? My mother is a happy person to live with; we are poor and our clothes are patched,—and sometimes they aren't even patched,—and I suppose she's a poor manager, but I am so glad she is because, when we do clean, it's because we want to and not to fight it day and night.' All through this day that's been so busy, when people have knocked at our door on one pretext or another, I've been waiting. All day Roger hasn't been to see me; it doesn't seem possible that he can be angry at me or stay away from me like this; it doesn't seem possible that he shouldn't understand me. I'm going up to-night to Oscar's Leap. It seemed to me that all the world had his voice to-day. Whenever I heard people talk far off, it seemed to me that I heard Roger; every time some one knocked on the door my heart leaped and I thought: 'He's coming at last.' Twice I walked uptown looking for him, and once there was a real errand,—not a make-believe one like when I was a little girl and wanted to do something that took me up to Aunt Sarah's; Aunt Sarah herself sent me, and how my ears were strained for the sound of his voice, and there was no sound at all in all the house. Then I did a thing that was very bold. I sat down at the piano and opened it and played and began to sing, hoping he would hear me, while I waited for the sewing for which Aunt Sarah had sent me. Then I heard footsteps on the stair and I knew that they weren't Roger's, but yet it seemed to me they must be—so much I wanted to see him that the very desire of my heart must call him to me—but no. I wonder what has happened; I wonder if he's angry; I wonder if he's hurt. I couldn't even ask Martha a word about him; I had to keep my mouth closed. It is partly my fault that we have to skulk in this way. It seems a curious thing that Martha should know if Roger was in the house somewhere. But surely he couldn't have been in the house or he would have come down when he heard me sing. Why should I feel ashamed at having tried to make him hear me? If I can go and call Alec from outside his house, why is it more wrong for me to go and call for the one whom I shall love all my days, and yet somehow I feel that I shouldn't. There is some deep instinct in me that makes me know I was wrong."

I suppose it was because of Ellen's absorption in Roger that she failed to write an aspect of these days that stand out to me as one of the charming memories of my girlhood, for it so sums up our New England society of that day. My grandmother had performed the kind office of announcing the betrothal to Miss Sarah, and this good woman's reply was characteristic.

"Well," said she, "trust Emily to get into mischief when Ellen gives us a moment's pause, and what irritates me the most, Sophia, is that I am not even allowed my just moment of anger. If I sulk, then there will be talk, to be sure, so I've got to go out and countenance this marriage of those 'babes of grace' as though it had been my fondest hope. I, forsooth, have got to go around and smile until my jaws are fairly dislocated to prevent the magpie chattering that there'll be; but before my anger cools I'm going down to give Emily a piece of my mind. When you consider her refusing a decent, advantageous marriage, and then becoming sentimental at her time of life, it's enough to make one's blood boil."

Miss Sarah eased her mind by making remarks like this to her sister and then said she: —

"Sophia Hathaway and I are going to bring our sewing and spend the afternoon, because you'll see that half the town will be here to find out what's happened."

So there we were, my grandmother and I, Mrs. Payne, Ellen, and Aunt Sarah — a solid phalanx.

"We'll answer," Miss Sarah announced, "no questions except those asked us."

Deacon Archibald and his wife were the first to call. The deacon came in cheerily, rubbing his hands.

"It was such a fine day," said Mrs. Archibald, "that we thought we'd repay the many visits that we owe."

"Yes, we are always so remiss in that," chirped Deacon Archibald.

"Won't you be seated? Take this more comfortable chair," said little Mrs. Payne.

"The weather's been fine lately," remarked the deacon.

"A fine summer, indeed, for the crops," agreed Miss Sarah; "the tobacco's doing splendidly in the valley."

There came another rap on the door and Mrs. Snow was admitted.

"I thought I'd run in just a moment to see if you had that mantle pattern," she said.

Mrs. Butler, stiff with rheumatism, came next. A knock was heard at the back door and I heard her heavy breathing and her "Well, Ellen, I just ran over to return your mother's hoe that Alec left at my house when he hoed my potatoes for me, but why he can't take back the tools himself I can't see. Has your mother got company; invited company, I mean?—because, Land Sakes! I can hear she's got company. I'm not deaf."

The question that they all longed to ask lay heavy in the air. It was good and bona-fide gossip that they had heard as coming direct from Mr. Sylvester himself, but so afraid is New England of making a mistake and of committing itself, that two other ladies had dropped in on an errand of one sort or another, or for calls, before Miss Sarah took advantage of a little pause in the conversation to remark:—

"I suppose every one of you here has come to find out if my sister is to marry Mr. Sylvester."

There was a little, fluttering chorus of dissent.

"Nonsense," said Miss Sarah, "I know what you wish to ask and what a bushel more will come to ask before the evening is over, and that's why I'm staying here; and tell every one that you meet that we shall be happy to tell them ourselves that such, indeed, is the happy fact."

Miss Sarah spoke with a large and grim geniality, for she always had the air of one who says, "Mankind, I am about to chastise you for your weakness, but I realize that I am human as well as you."

Meantime my poor Ellen had heard in each one of these knocks on the door Roger's knock, and so she continued to hear the next day. She wrote:—

"He's gone away, and I have only learned about it by chance. Just by chance I heard Aunt Sarah saying: 'As if it wasn't excitement enough to have this happen yesterday, that young scallawag gets up and leaves me at a moment's notice.' Two of his friends came through, it seems, and Roger left with them. He left without sending word or sending me any message. He says he's gone for a day or two only. Aunt Sarah says she would not be surprised if he never came back, but that can't happen. How could it happen? Did he think that I had failed him so that he doesn't want me any more, or that I lacked so in courage and in love of him?... Another day has gone and no word from him. I don't think I've ever felt so alone in all my life and so cut off from all human help. I know it is wicked of me, but mother's happiness hurts me. I want her to be happy, but oh! it hurts me to watch it. I wish I could go off by myself somewhere, and yet I know that there I will be worse than I am now, with a thousand small things to do to somehow fill up the days. Something must have happened to him. I watch myself like some other person for fear I shall seem sad for a moment, for if I do it will look as though I am not pleased about my mother. Oh! I hope that I won't hurt their joy in any way. I wonder how women live who have to wait long for news of those they love. I seem to move around in the world, but I really do nothing but wait. Each time I see my aunt I think that she will have news of him; I'm grateful to her now if she only tells me he hasn't come. When I am asleep, I'm still listening and waiting for him. Something must have happened to him, because he must want to see me as I do him. It seems to me that no one could hurt any one they loved as much as this and be alive."

Here it was for the first time that Ellen tasted that bitter pain of women, waiting. It sometimes seems to me that this is an anguish in which we live and of which men know nothing. During the course of a long life every woman passes so many hours of still agony when she must fold her hands and smile and wait. We cannot go out seeking the beloved, but must sit and wait until he comes. Like Ellen, when you have had a misunderstanding it is not yours to run generously forward; you can't clap your hat on your head and say, "Here, I'll make an end to this; I'll go and find her." No, you must sit waiting for the sound of his footsteps coming toward you; wait until your whole soul is tense; wait until each sound is part of this hope deferred. All women know this pain of waiting; and when our time of waiting for a sweetheart is over, the sons we love go out into the world, and again we can do nothing but sit still and wait for news of the travelers, wait for the little, scant messages of love which their careless hands pen to us in some casual moment. The long days pass and the letters don't come, and still we wait. We sit and wait for our children to be born, through the long months, with the black certainty of the birth that may be death staring us in the face.

Some women get used to waiting. I think that those who do have closed the doors of their hearts to the keener range of feeling, having suffered so much that they say to themselves, "Here, I'll suffer no longer." There are yet others who pass through the pain of waiting, going by this thorny, bleeding, silent road of doubt and pain to a higher acquiescence. It is a long way there, and the heart of us must weep much in silence before we can attain this glorified peace. I have known the spirits of women to snap like the overstrained strings of a harp, as they waited with smiles upon their lips.

I am sorry sometimes for all women, and most of all for the impatient, tender, and flaming spirits of young girls who meet this pain for the first time.

It is because we have all suffered in this way that the most generous among us run so eagerly to meet those whom they love. Having tasted this pain, we wish forevermore to spare others anything like it. The more shallow-hearted and, perhaps, wiser women, and those who are not children of light, having tasted it, use the anguish of suspense as a weapon in the everlasting warfare between man and woman. But there is hardly a woman grown who could not echo the cry of Ellen when she wrote:—

"I do not dare to go out of the house for fear I might miss some word of him, and yet how can I stay in the house knowing my own thoughts? I wish to fill the gray horror of these empty hours with anything that the wayside will bring me; I want to go out and play with the children; I want to find Alec and walk with him. I try to remember just one thing—that some time to-day or to-morrow, or the next day, I shall hear something. This can't go on forever; there has to come an end."

CHAPTER XVII

I, with my eyes fastened on the romance of Mrs. Payne and Mr. Sylvester, had noticed nothing; the explanation that Roger had gone off for a few days with friends was enough for me; but it was Alec, with a keener vision, who had seen something wrong.

"What ails Ellen?" he had asked me.

"Why—what should?" I asked.

"Roberta," said Alec, "is Ellen in love with Roger?"

"How should I know?" said I.

Alec looked down, kicking the dust before him with the gesture of a little boy.

"It would be natural if they cared for each other," he continued. Then he suddenly flung out his hand and said, "If it's so, he won't ever make her happy."

"Why, Alec, what do you mean?" I said.

"He's only thinking about himself; he's interested only in Roger Byington," Alec declared with vehemence.

He filled these next days as full of himself as he could; making Ellen laugh at his fantastic goings-on as he pretended to be the bulletin which announced how far the gossip had reached. With his tender second sight he tried to hide Ellen from herself or whatever it was that was troubling her.

As Ellen said, the trouble couldn't last forever, and the end came unexpectedly. While we were sitting in the orchard I saw Ellen's hand go to her heart and her face change color; she sat still a lovely, quivering thing, with all the soul of her running out to meet Roger, and he advanced through the sweet clover, swishing at it with a little cherry wand that he had cut when walking. He had gone away a fairy prince—his only fault had been loving Ellen too much—and he came back a naughty little boy. Even I noticed the change in him. There was an arrogant, willful tilt to his head which belied the lightness of his disarming manner, and one which said: "First I'll try to coax you into good humor, but beware of my stubbornness if you find fault with me too far." He was the male that will not admit that he has faults. "Be thankful that I'm back at all," was what his bearing implied; "and we'll ignore also that I've been away, if you please."

Ellen, poor child, had no idea of blaming him, any more than she had an instinct of hiding her emotions. Never once had she blamed Roger, even to herself, for going away, and at the sudden end of her suspense uncontrollable tears came to her eyes. Men have written books about the folly of the tears of women. Who knows it better than they, poor things? There are uncontrollable women, of course, who are as spendthrift with tears as some men of anger. Tears like these of Ellen's are as unexpected and uncontrollable as a sudden storm, and I, knowing what it meant when Ellen cried, left them quickly.

Ellen wrote about it:—

"Oh, the unspeakable shame of having cried. I didn't know I was going to; I haven't cried since he has been away; I've only waited. He was sweet and tender with me, but he said whimsically: 'You, too, Ellen! I've had many a tearful home-coming with my mother. If one stays away unexpectedly from women, no matter who they are, the first thing they do when you turn up again is to find fault with you or else weep over you.' Then he held me out at arm's length. 'Ellen, you're not going to make of me the sinner that repented.' I don't know what leaden weight I have in my heart; it seems all so different; it's like a little, commonplace squabble. I'm always disappointing him; he has thought me different from all other women and I would so like to be, but I am just the same. He didn't even refer to the cause of his going away. We talked of this and that and couldn't find each other. He looked at me curiously two or three times and said, 'Ellen, I thought I should never see tears in your eyes.'"

Here, indeed, was a shifting of base; they had been playing the higher harmonies that men and women play together; their spirits had been in perfect unison; even the tragic parting had had its undercurrent of understanding, and now here they were with their feet on earth; Ellen with homesick eyes for the land of lost content and Roger with a little sneer that she should have let him see that she had no pride against him. Her absence of coquetry was her undoing. He knew now he could put her down or take her up at will, and her price was a few tears. Her spirit stood out in that moment of welcome, shining and naked, her little shy spirit, the reflection of whose light alone had been enough for Alec.

From the point of view of age, it is Roger for whom I am sorry, for with all courage and charm and ability and the swift, pulsing flow of life in him, life had tainted him already so that this ultimate gift of herself made him think Ellen too easy of attainment. The situation was one that had been repeated time and time again, sometimes by men and sometimes by women. Roger had had his naughtiness and his lack of consideration and his sudden and impatient vanishing out of a difficult situation treated by tears and reproaches. Poor Ellen, by her very innocence, had trodden a path of the emotion familiar to him, since his way out of difficulties had been a sudden impatient vanishing. If she could have only had the inspired sense to have taken his return in a matter-of-course manner, it would have piqued him, and again Ellen would have won; but how play sorry games like this with the best beloved? One of the sad things of love is that it is in absurd and trivial ways like this that it falls from its highest state and loses its radiance.

From the account of her journal they jogged along a few days at a slack-water; Ellen groping forever for Roger, Roger a little bored at the too-eagerly offered heart; their positions oddly reversed; Roger rather magnificently forgiving Ellen for having annoyed him.

Then suddenly into this doldrums of the emotions burst Miss Grant. A flaming affection is hard to hide. It shines like a light behind a closed door,—let two people walk ever so carefully. Now the eyes of one follow the other and the look is a caress; now some one intercepts an exchange of glances, and that exchange means, to any one whose heart has beat fast for love, a promise of everlasting devotion; you see a girl's hand steal to her fast-beating heart, or the young man waiting for her with that aching impatience of the young.

So gossip had begun about Roger and Ellen. Some one had seen them walking down the street so absorbed that they had seen no one else; another had noticed Ellen walking across the bridge to the mountain and Roger going before her. Little by little the people who had separately observed these things had talked together until between them they had pieced together from broken fragments the whole story, and then, like a picture thrown unexpectedly on the screen, the gossip of it came to Miss Grant.

I suppose she had gotten bits of it before, hints and innuendoes, of the kind people give who are too pusillanimous to face a woman like Miss Sarah with a point-blank question. The whole thing was focused one afternoon when she had said lightly to Mrs. Snow that she didn't know where on earth Roger had passed his time in such a quiet little town.

"Well, Sarah, if you spent more time down at Emily's, perhaps you'd know."

To Miss Sarah's hot, "What do you mean?" —

"I mean that wherever Ellen is, Roger's apt to be, and no reason making such big eyes at me; a very nice sort of thing, I think it."

Miss Sarah merely put on her bonnet and shawl and marched majestically down the hill. She found Ellen on the back porch, in the midst of a foam of ruffles she was hemming for her mother's gown. She towered above Ellen, an avenging fate, whose gray curls bobbed on each side of her head.

"Ellen, what's this gossip I hear about you and Roger?" she demanded. Before Ellen had time to reply, as though she read her confession in the color that mounted to her face, "How could you do such a thing, Ellen?" she fumed. "Don't you know that Roger Byington came here to work and settle down; don't you know that he has a marriage already planned? Don't you see the position you've put your family in, that of snatching at the fortune of an old friend! A fortune that's destined elsewhere, and that we were bound, you as well as I, to guard! You've been deceiving the whole of us!"

Ellen rose to her feet and faced her, her sewing still in her hands, the blue ruffles around her white frock like a wave of the sea.

"I've deceived no one, Aunt Sarah," said she, with a touch of sternness in her voice, and just here Roger appeared.

He had heard voices, and had heard his and Ellen's names mentioned, and he had then seen Miss Grant storming down the hill like some aged New England Valkyrie and had followed her. He arrived in time around the side of the house to catch her last words, and the flaming anger that any one should scold his Ellen blew away forever the flatness that had for a moment assailed them.

He threw his arms around Ellen as though he would protect her from everything for all time. "Miss Grant," he said, "the reason I'm here in this town is Ellen. I walked through here one time and I saw Ellen and talked with her for a few minutes by the roadside, and so I came back. No one else I've ever seen in life matters to me—nothing else but Ellen matters. Please remember that if I amount to anything ever, it will be because of Ellen, and if I fail, it will be because I have failed Ellen. Had I had my way Ellen would not have been here now with you; she'd be married to me."

Ellen wrote:—

> "I don't know what it did to me to have it talked about in the open. I felt as if I belonged forever to Roger, as though some way this outward profession of faith of his brought out and made positive everything that he had said and that I had felt, and that we truly belonged to one another."

The old lady measured the young people with an angry gaze.

"Young man," said she, "I consider you've abused my hospitality; you have put me and my brother and my whole family in a false light before your parents. You entangle yourself in sentimentalities with a married woman, you play false with your sweetheart, and when your father wishes you to reconstruct your life, you throw them both over and place me in the position of having seemed to connive at a marriage with my niece. I shall write your mother my disapproval by the next post, and if Ellen knew as much of your past history as I do, she wouldn't take this sudden infatuation seriously, and if she had any dignity she would withdraw at once from this false position."

"Your letter," Roger replied with some heat, "will reach my mother somewhat after my own. When Ellen's love for her mother overcame her better judgment and she refused to go with me, I wrote my mother on my return as I told her I would do; and now, permit me, Miss Grant, to withdraw from your house which will save your pride in this matter."

It was an old-fashioned quarrel that Youth and Age indulged in, and Ellen's journal gives more of it, full of stately words and innuendo and recriminations cloaked in fine-sounding periods, and I think both Roger and Miss Sarah enjoyed their own rhetoric heartily.

Mrs. Payne heard the noise of the combat, and when Miss Sarah realized that her sister had been, as she said, "an accomplice," her indignation knew no bounds, though she admitted:—

"I'll do you justice, Emily; you've so little common sense that I don't suppose for a moment you thought of anything but the sentimentality of this ill-governed young man and your Ellen. You didn't, I suppose, for a moment consider that Ellen is not the sort of a marriage planned for him by his father."

Mrs. Payne's wide-eyed, "Why shouldn't she be? Ellen's so sweet and pretty," collapsed the older lady's anger like a pricked balloon, as nothing else could have done. Ellen's picture of her is this: "Aunt Sarah flopped down, she didn't sit, and gathered her draperies around her like a wounded Roman matron."

Roger, at Mrs. Payne's words, again put his arm around Ellen and laughed aloud. He adored their unworldliness. The bad little boy in him vanished; so did the man of the world who cannot bear generosity in the beloved. He spoke truly enough when he said all the best things in him ran out ahead of him to meet Ellen. He said to Miss Sarah gently:—

"You see, we really care for each other, Aunt Sarah, and I'm awfully sorry about putting you in a false position, but that doesn't count very much compared to Ellen's and my happiness, does it?

Please believe me when I tell you that your side of this never occurred to me and so I'll take myself away to-night." The moment of high-sounding periods was over.

"Hadn't you better stay?" asked Miss Sarah. "Think of the talk, Roger."

"I want talk," he said,—"all the talk in the world; I would like everybody to know how I care for Ellen—I welcome gossip."

> "The way he laughed"—wrote Ellen—"made one feel the way Spring looks; I was so proud, and wondered more than ever what I could have done to have any one like Roger love me."

During the days when they had been at odds with life, they had taken pains to have me with them; it was the first time that they had shown themselves eager for my company together. I had been confidante first for Ellen and then for Roger, and then again for Ellen, but seldom had I seen them both at once. Now, after this explanation with Miss Grant, they unconsciously thrust me aside with no more regard for me than if I had been a withered flower. I was going to Ellen's to help with the sewing. I had left her a little lack-luster, a little wistful; Roger had been sulky and inclined to cynicism; and now they swept down on me like a splendid young god and goddess, no longer making any effort to keep the town in ignorance; they took it in in a magnificent gesture, the way they looked at each other; shouted it aloud, and, as though to carry out in very truth the words he had spoken to Miss Grant when he said he would like to shout through the town that he loved Ellen, he took her hand in his when he saw me and swung it to and fro; and in my day such an action as this was one which would cause the quiet windows to bristle with interrogatory eyes. You might be perfectly sure that there would be quiet slippings through back doors and gossiping under grape arbors.

That evening I met Roger coming down the street and he stopped to tell me:—

"We've had it out with Aunt Sarah, and both Aunt Sarah and I

94

have written to my mother. Now we'll soon have an end to this shilly-shallying."

"And if your parents don't like it?"

"God help them if they don't," he said. "Any parents I have will have to like it."

And there was so sinister a note in his voice that I shivered. Sometimes when he spoke there was a weight to a light word that seemed like a heavy wind.

It was not long before the town had more to talk about. Mrs. Byington, in her beautiful and fashionable clothes, was as conspicuous as though she had come riding in a palanquin. The city and country were much more apart in those days, and home-made patterns taken from some remote city ones were passed from hand to hand; dolls dressed in Boston still carried the mode somewhat; and in our honest village, loveliness was put by with youth, and lovely was the quality of Mrs. Byington. At fifty she was tall and slender, her hair a little gray, her neck graceful like a girl's; she walked swayingly, and age was not a quality with which she seemed to have reckoned. With the changing years she had a quality as compelling as youth itself, and this without the slightest attempt at seeming less than her years.

Ellen writes:—

"Roger's mother came to see me alone, and before her, so beautiful and soft, I felt as though I had been made yesterday. It happened that I opened the door for her, and I knew who she was and she knew me, for she said: 'Dear child, I know you are Ellen; I wanted to come by myself.' She looked at me with searching eyes that were a little sad, and all of a sudden I felt very sorry for her, for it must be very hard, when you have a son that you love, to learn all at once that his life belongs to some one else. We sat down and talked a little, and my heart beat so that I could hardly say anything, and I felt that I was very stupid, and that if Roger could be there he wouldn't like the way I was acting, and all of a sudden she put her arms around me and kissed me, and said: 'Dear Ellen, you are very lovely and very perfect, and, indeed, I knew you would be very "something" to send my wild Roger after you at such a rate. You love him very much, don't you?' I couldn't speak, and only bowed my head; and she said, as though talking to herself rather than to me, 'Poor child, it would be better for you if you loved him less; he would be more yours.' I asked her what she meant. She thought a moment, and then said: 'Perhaps you'll never find out; you're so sweet, Ellen; even Roger wouldn't hurt a child.' And for a moment I felt a little flaming anger at her for not understanding him better. I wanted to tell her that there was only sweetness in Roger for those who knew how to find it, but, of course, I didn't dare. There was something in her tone that made a cold shadow fall over me."

It seemed as though all difficulties were cleared from before them, when Ellen found herself face to face with what really was the first important issue of this time. After all, the things in love that count are not all the obstacles imposed on us from without. It is strange to me why people have always written of these rather than of those far more important moments, as when, for instance, one first sees the beloved face to face as he really is. Love for a moment makes us transcend ourselves, and Roger was a brave lover, and Ellen had known nothing of him except Roger the lover, when suddenly she caught a new glimpse of Roger. She wrote:—

"I don't know what I'm going to do—nothing I suppose. I've seen Roger angry with his mother. It was our last afternoon all together and she was talking very seriously with us. She said: 'Your Ellen is very sweet, Roger. Keep her happiness, and if you play fast and loose again, you deserve all the unhappiness the world can bring you.' She has wanted me to see him as he is, and has talked around the edges of this, and she said to me, 'I came here wondering who you were, Ellen, and ever since I saw you I've been wondering what Roger will do to you in this new life of yours begun so sweetly.' One time she cried out, 'Oh! why do women have to marry men?' And then she laughed at herself for saying it. Ever since she came Roger has been watching her. He's had a critical attitude and is ready to find fault at a moment's notice. It was as if the impatience of the whole week overflowed. What he said wasn't so much. Oh! he kept within bounds before me, but the restrained anger of his manner was as though he had struck her, as though he had hurt her, as though the force of his anger would throw her from the room. She held up her head a little proudly, but she only said, as though to bring him to himself, 'Roger, Roger!' warning him, one would think, not to lose further control of himself. She spoke as if she were used to this wounding, terrible manner, a manner that gets its own way in spite of everything; and I stood there trembling inside, and I began thinking, 'Who are you, Roger, and who am I?' Now it is all at once as if I had an answer to why she seemed to pity me, as though she wanted to protect me from everything. All my instinct is to run and hide in some place where I shall hide from him forever. I know nothing of him or he of me."

CHAPTER XVIII

There comes a moment in the life of almost every one when, bewildered, for the first time they meet an everyday and faulty person in place of the beloved. Sometimes this is the beginning of a long disillusion; it is then that many find out that one has not been in love at all, but only in love with being in love. With young lovers one often calls this first glimpse the first quarrel. After marriage this slow torment of becoming accustomed to another personality in the body of the beloved is called the "time of adjustment."

With Ellen this moment was a severe spiritual crisis. As she had seen concentrated in the last weeks only the lovable things in Roger, so in this one moment she had a vision of all in him that was inimical to happiness and peace. It was as if that blind, voiceless judge that sits deep within all of us and bids us love, hate, or fear, had been aroused to its depth, and its final judgment of Roger had been that here was danger. Had there been any place to run to, she would have fled, but there was nothing to do but sit still. She dreamed at night that she saw his face savage in anger, heartless in its desire, and relentless in its will to get what it wanted from life; and since she could not leave home to run away from him, she ran from him spiritually.

When he came to see her next, he could hardly find Ellen in the inert and docile person who presented herself to his gaze. It was as though the glance he had given his mother and the tone in which he had spoken had been to her a prophecy of life to come. She saw him with that terrible clairvoyance that love gives; she saw clearly what her life in the hands of this other Roger would mean; and it seemed as if the very inner spirit of her struggled to free herself from his power.

I, personally, fear the shocks of the spirit as some fear physical pain, and instinctively I withdrew from the perversities of men, and I now look shudderingly back on two marriages which I might have made but for this warning bell which rang over the reefs of the spirit.

Her first movement had been one of flaming indignation; that burned out, leaving behind it the ashes of a dull, apathetic fear. When he asked her what was the matter and why, she told him she was afraid of him. He called himself a brute, he apologized to his mother, but she remained inert and docile, as aloof as a person who has been stunned by the spectacle of a great disaster, and, indeed, the flood of her emotions had ebbed back violently.

In despair Roger came to me.

"I've lost Ellen," he told me. "We've awfully bad tempers in our family, and my mother didn't understand that since I've known Ellen there are a whole lot of things in my life that I want to forget. The me Ellen knows is a different me from the one mother knows."

He had never been as sweet to Ellen as he was now. She had seen before a brave lover who rushed everything before him and when he was refused anything would turn into a naughty little boy. Now he was a tender suppliant asking for mercy, confessing his sins and inventing sweet and touching things to do for Ellen. I think the men of my day were crueler as men and warmer as lovers. A man like Roger possessed himself more of a woman's mind and life than the men of to-day that I see around me seem able to do with their sweethearts. There was no little corner of her spirit that he did not wish to occupy, and to gain admission to her frightened little heart he made himself small and humble and appealing. Of the sincerity of his wretchedness and his repentance there was no doubt.

"If she were only angry with me," he said to me, "but she's afraid, Roberta. It's a terrible thing to see her shrink from me. She doesn't mean to be unkind. She told me in all seriousness, as if she meant it, that she thought it would be better for all of us if I left her now. Why, she's my life, Roberta!"

I was profoundly touched, as who would not have been? Nor did I fail to repeat this to Ellen. I had told Alec what the matter was, for seeing Ellen listless and remote he had jumped to the conclusion that Roger had hurt her in some way, and in Roger's defense I told him the truth and he put himself stolidly on the side of Ellen's instinct. Through one long day she and Alec went off together as they had when they were children, while Roger raged up and down. Ellen wrote:—

"We played, as we did when I was little, 'Two Years Ago,' and for one, beautiful afternoon I forgot how life can hurt. Just toward the end Alec cried out to me, 'Oh, Ellen, why can't I be older! Why couldn't it have been I? I'd never have hurt you, I'd never have made you afraid of me.' And I know that's true, and I know, too, that poor Alec could never find a key to the place in me that could be hurt. There's something wrong with women, for when once one has felt one's pulse beat fast, one can never again be content with a sweet and kind affection. One must wish forevermore to drown one's self forever and to let the waters of life sweep over one's head, however bitter they may be."

Already, though she didn't know it, she was coming back to Roger. Every day he went to see her with some carefully thought-out little gift. Every night he wrote her a letter which he sent by me, and she wrote in answer a letter that she didn't send.

"I suppose [she writes to Roger] that we can only be cured of the worst hurts of all by those who have hurt us. Oh, please hide me from yourself! Oh, protect me! from this Roger, since I am so afraid of you that my whole spirit shudders away from you. Shield me from this, or let me go now while I yet have strength to leave you, or else make me forget forever how black life could be if I ever saw again the face that you turned then on your mother, and that yet was a part of you."

There is nothing truer in the life of the affections than this, that the wound made by those whom we love can only be cured by them. One may be sick even to death, and yet the only cure can come from the one who has poisoned life for us. There is only one other way to cure the hurt, and that is to stop loving. That's why a great many things become easier to bear as the years go by. We find men and women philosophically facing situations which formerly would have stopped all life for them. These are the dead of heart who have forgotten to care when they do this, and where one woman gains peace from a higher understanding of the man she loves, a dozen others find it by ceasing to love at all.

Ellen made her attempt at escape, and then came back because she couldn't help it. The one person in the world who could have helped her was Alec. She was sincere when she told me:—

"If Alec was my brother, and had a home for me somewhere where I need not see Roger again, I'd go to him."

It was her very docility and lack of resistance that maddened Roger. He told me:—

"Somehow Ellen has slipped out of my hands into a magic circle; she's afraid of me. It's as though she lived inside a crystal shell—I can see her and speak to her, but I can't touch her."

I, myself, was very much disturbed and moved by it all. There was Ellen who had burned in a fire of happiness, whose very look at Roger had been a caress, who seemed to give herself to him by the way she stood,—her arms relaxed as though all her body cried out to him to take her,—now lost in apathy; nothing that I told her affected her as far as I could see. After days of this, just as I was giving up hope, I met them one afternoon, swinging down the street toward me, with the air of a god and goddess recently let out of prison. Roger had Prudentia flung on his shoulder, and carried the child aloft as though she were a flag of triumph. All the explanation I ever had of the reconciliation was what I had then and there.

"He came down the street," Ellen told me, "with Prudentia on his shoulder, and said, 'Hello, Ellen,' and I said, 'Hello, Roger,' and he put out his hand to me and I took it. Why, Roberta, aren't you glad?" asked Ellen.

"She wanted more pomp and circumstance," Roger jeered at me. "She wanted you, Ellen, to rush to my arms and say, 'Roderigo, I forgive thee.'"

They went on; I heard their laughter down the street. That was all the thanks they gave me.

CHAPTER XIX

Ellen wiped the memory of their misunderstanding completely from her mind. If she had cared for Roger before, now she burned her bridges behind her; she swamped herself in her devotion to him. He stayed in our town until late fall, and during these months he seemed to want no other thing than the companionship of Ellen. The hours that he spent in work every day were their tragedy. In her journal Ellen prattled of a time "when they should be married and she could be with him even when he was working."

"The world is full now," she complained, "of closed doors and good-nights and good-byes."

All the diverse and many-sided problems of marriage resolved themselves, in her simple mind, into one single meaning, and that was the continual presence of Roger. She passed the hours away from him drowned in the thought of him. Though at that time she wrote very little in her journal,—she was happy,—she did write a series of little, good-night letters that were like so many kisses, fond and extravagant, the happy babblings of a perfectly happy heart. Meantime Roger was studying. It was the first time he had applied himself to work and found the power of his mind. In the quiet of this town he got into a tremendous stride of work and ate up books before him as fire licks up brushwood. They spent a great deal of their time together, planning his future and talking how great a man he was going to be. He had a gift of natural eloquence and loved an audience at any time. In that New England fall, when the crisp air is like wine and the hills are a miracle of color, Roger brooded over the picture of his own future, sketching outlines which he afterwards filled out. By letter he made friends again with his father.

Their engagement had been announced and Ellen was given the consideration which a good marriage brings one in a little village, a consideration which she didn't even notice. Mildred Dilloway, in the mean time, had been—in the homely New England phrase—"keeping company" with Edward Graham, and no one was surprised when it became known that they were to be married. Ellen writes in connection with this:—

"When I think of what a little fool I was at that time, I could beat my head against the door. If I could have but looked ahead a little, I would have had a little more sense. I needn't have listened at all to Edward's blitherings and been saved two years of discomfort. Edward himself told me about it. 'Do not think, Ellen,' he said, 'that I'm unfaithful to the thought of you.' 'You couldn't be,' said I. 'You'll always be poetry to me, remember that,' he told me. 'I shall try to forget it,' said I. I have never before wished to throw something at any one as I did then. It was easy to see that he was a little disappointed in himself that he could care for any one else after having made so great a fuss and mourned around so. I wish he would go away, because I hate to be forever reminded of the me that used to be. What if one should turn back into the person that one was once? I wonder who the person is that I'm going to be. It will be a happy person or else I shan't be alive; because if I have Roger I shall be happy, and if anything happens to him it will happen to me, too."

At that moment in her life she could not imagine any other separation from him than that caused by some disaster. She hadn't even faced the necessity of his leaving her when winter came. She knew he was going away, but she didn't realize it. They drifted along, making more of a drama all the time of the inevitable good-nights and the inevitable separations. As Ellen wrote: "People who are in love should be endowed; there isn't time for anything else."

During this little perfect time life held its breath until Roger went away. The end came quite suddenly, with a peremptory letter from his father, who had a chance for him to enter a very well-known law office, under advantageous circumstances. While the shadow of separation was over them, it was like a cloud that passes near by and only bade the sunshine in which they stood more bright. She knew Roger was going, but she didn't really believe it. She wrote:—

"I lived through months of learning to realize he was gone between the time he left and dinner. Mr. Sylvester was there, and for a time I had to put aside the selfishness of my own grief and I was glad to forget it in talking of one little thing after another, the way one does to stifle down the pain of the heart. I wanted to run after Roger and look at his face once more. I wanted to run after him and foolishly throw myself in front of the horse and say, 'You can't go.' The part of me that talks was gay, because deeper than anything else was the wish in me to speed him joyfully and to have his last memory of me a gay and triumphant one. Time is a strange thing; all day it's walked along like a funeral procession, and before this it has been going so fast that there has hardly been a chance to get a word in edgewise between the striking of the hours; and since Roger went it's taken an eternity for it to strike the next quarter. I've tried to comfort myself by going up to Oscar's Leap, but my heart was so heavy that I could hardly walk all of the beautiful, weary way. I don't like myself for writing like this, for I have him and he really loves me. The more I see people and listen to the things they say, the more I am sure that very few people really love any one, and those who do love are seldom loved in return. It must be a terrible thing to love and feel one's self unloved. Now I'm going to get ready for my mother's wedding and then get ready for mine, and while my mind tells me I must be good, my heart cries out, 'Oh! Why can't I trade off the useless weeks at the other end of my life for the weeks that would mean so much now!' As he went away from me, I felt as though I were never going to see him again, and, indeed, this Roger and this Ellen will never see each other again. It seems to me that before he comes again I shall be made old by waiting, the days crawl past so slow and leaden-footed. I've said good-bye to this most beautiful time when I've said good-bye to Roger."

At first he wrote her very often, but briefly. She wrote to him, in the intimacy of the letters she did not intend to send:—

"Your dear letters mean, 'I love you, Ellen; I think of you; my heart goes out to you.' Once in a while they say, 'I thirst for you,' but they tell me nothing of all the many things that I hunger so to know. I'd like to be able to see your life and know what time you wake up, what time you go to your office, and how your office looks, and which way it is set toward the sun so I could imagine you moving around, and you don't even answer my little, discreet questions. I would like to know the faces of all the people you meet often and how you amuse yourself. I wonder have you lost Ellen in your big and fearsome city. Roger, I have times when I'm afraid, and I don't know of what— just fear, as though the inner heart of me rang, 'Something's wrong, something's wrong, something's wrong,' where my mind has nothing to go on. Roger, I wait for each one of your letters as if I was afraid it wouldn't come, and as if it were to be the last. I'm afraid. I don't trust life as I did, and when I don't trust life, I can't find you; when I trust life, it's as if when I shut my eyes I can put out my hand and touch you. But lately it is as though I wander around in the dark looking for you. I tell myself it's foolish, but my heart won't listen to the voice of reason. It is as though my confidence had been taken away from me, as though it had been a gift no one could touch with hands. My mother's wedding doesn't mean to me any more her happiness, but the day that you shall come back to me and give me back my confidence in life, and when I look on you again I shall know that everything is well in the world. I know that nothing has happened and that nothing can happen, but my heart knows differently."

CHAPTER XX

During the winter Alec came home from college every Saturday, walking over the mountain each Saturday afternoon for fifteen miles, and going back Monday morning by a stage that started at some unearthly hour, and carried passengers over to the nearest town to us through which a railroad ran in those days.

Various boys of those he had around him would straggle down the road to meet him, so when he came into the town on cold winter nights it was with an escort of red-nosed, red-tippeted and booted youngsters.

This was before any of the new forms of education for boys had even so much as stirred in their sleep, and the town agreed in considering Alec's friendship with the youngsters a waste of time on both sides: the parents of the boys saying that they had something better to do—in filling the wood-boxes for instance—than to tramp out and get their toes frozen off to meet Alec. Alec's friends, on the other hand, wondered what he wanted with a "parcel of young ones." It was only Ellen and myself who caught a glimpse of just what it was that Alec was accomplishing, when we also would walk out to meet him. Besides supplying them in his own person with a hero to worship, he drew them out and untangled their knotty minds for them; for the boy of ten and twelve was, in my girlhood, even more misunderstood and kicked about and generally at odds with life than he is now. Nothing was done to make his school days happier or the path of learning easier. Teachers, almost without exception, were the boys' natural enemies. Almost all the communication boys had from older people in my day, besides religious instructions, were recommendations to get to work and to get to work quickly.

These snowy walks in the crisp air to meet Alec were the punctuation points of our lives, and the long, pleasant Saturday evenings that we spent together, with perhaps some of the other young people dropping in, were our greatest pleasure. I am sure Ellen's house seemed to him the gayest place in the world, because we concentrated into those few hours on Saturday evening the gayety of the whole week, though Ellen did not have much time for "mulling," as her aunt called it. Getting ready for her mother's marriage meant not only the preparation of her clothes, but also the preparation of the whole Scudder house for its occupancy by Mr. Sylvester and Matilda, Flavilla, and Prudentia.

Ellen's mood was not at all consistent with that of vague apprehension, and this warning note of her spirit she failed to listen to most of the time; as long as Roger's letters came regularly, she lived in a shimmering world of imagination, writing to him all the things she dared, and then writing to him again all the things she was too timid to tell him. All the outward details of her life were constant and pressing enough, and very homely, most of them; while within she lived in a shimmering world of her own, her lovely garden inclosed of the spirit, into which she let no unkind breath blow; and so her love for Roger blossomed throughout the long months of the winter. Then toward Easter came her mother's wedding, which meant to Ellen Roger's return. The Resurrection and Roger's return came all together in Ellen's mind.

When his letter came that told her he couldn't leave his office at this moment, she could not at first believe it, any more than she could at first believe that he had gone away.

Alec was there, and he asked me shortly:—

"Why couldn't Roger come?"

"He's busy," I said.

Alec gave me an odd look.

"One can do what one wants to," said he.

He was one of those over whom Love passes a maturing hand. At twenty he had lost the young-robin look of expression, just as he had lost early the puppy aspect that a boy has before he has gotten used to man-size hands and feet.

"It's hard," he said, "to sit back and do nothing. It's hard when you love any one as I do Ellen not to be able to get for her any of the things in life that she wants the most."

"What does she want," I asked, "that she hasn't?"

"Well," Alec reflected, "I can come to see her every week and Roger can't." He might have said: "I can spend my life on her and give her every thought of my heart and stand between her and unhappiness as much as I can, and Roger can't."

This was one of the few times that Ellen played make-believe to herself. I think she had to. It was only later that her straight mind said what Alec had said, "We can do what we want to." She hid her own disappointment from herself, and life was good to her in that it gave her a great deal to do. Although in those days wedding journeys were very rare, Mr. Sylvester had an old friend, a minister, near Washington, who came up to marry them and they were to exchange pulpits, and so directly after her disappointment Ellen was left alone with the three Sylvester children. Matilda at this time was already eleven and she remarked gravely to Ellen, — "Ellen, we've all decided that you can be our mother. Of course we shall call your mother 'Mother,' too, and we shall love her like that, because we've made up our minds that it is our duty," — Matilda was very particular about duty, — "but you'll be our real mother. I've done the best I can with the children," — for thus did Matilda always refer to her little sisters, — "but our clothes are in a terrible state since Mrs. Gillig went away." For the Sylvesters' housekeeper had gone promptly after the announcement of her employer's engagement. She had departed to the next town, where her relatives lived, saying that she was not going to stay around and be any one's "kill-joy"; so with an occasional day's work from Mrs. Butler and help from Ellen and me, they had gotten on as best they could.

> "I got their poor, little things unpacked [said Ellen] and got them their supper and put them to bed and Flavia patted my cheek and said, 'Ellen, you're so happy, that's why we love you,' and Prudentia said, 'Yes, I love folks that laugh,' and it came over me that for a while, anyway, I really am their mother—poor me, who knows so little about doing anything. Before I went to bed Matilda put her arm around me and said, 'Oh! Ellen, I want to grow up and be capable and take care of father and mother and everybody, and I've been just as capable as I know how ever since Mrs. Gillig left. I've been so capable it makes my

jaws ache, and I want to stop and be a little girl.' And pretty soon Aunt Sarah came in to see how badly I had done everything and to grumble good-naturedly over my endeavors, and then Grandma Hathaway dropped in to see if I needed anything, and they went off together and left Alec and me alone, and the children in bed. And Alec never once looked at me as though he cared for me; he was only funny and told me stories, just as if he knew I couldn't have borne affection from any one but Roger."

So it was that Ellen hid from herself and from the pain that was in her heart. This was one of the few times she played make-believe with herself. She was afraid of her own doubt and afraid of her own thoughts, really afraid for the first time; for this is another of the painful milestones which most of us have to pass in the long and bleeding road of love—the first time that we are afraid to face our fears.

Ellen and her mother had been buying cloth for Ellen's trousseau, and she had put it all by for her mother to begin on when her mother should be married. I was to help her, and so, of course, was Aunt Sarah.

In our days, girls mostly made their own trousseaux, and the richer among us had some seamstress engaged for a couple of months or six weeks, but friends helped one another, and one was supposed to go to one's husband with linen enough to last a long time in life, and with good, substantial garments, suitable for various occasions in a gentlewoman's life. Ellen had a poplin and a cashmere among other things, and when I came a day or two after her mother's wedding to encourage her to begin on her own things, I found her on her hands and knees cutting.

"Why, Ellen Payne! What's that you're doing?" For instead of cutting out one beautiful cashmere garment she was cutting three little frocks. "Oh, Miss Grant!" I exclaimed, scandalized, to Miss Sarah, "Ellen's cutting up her blue cashmere from her trousseau for the children."

Miss Grant adjusted her glasses and peered down at the patterns on the floor.

"Well, there," said she, "you have Ellen. We'll have Ellen Payne's trousseau walking all over town on three pairs of legs, and rather than patch up their old things, she begins her new life by taking the very trousseau off her own back! Some would think you were self-sacrificing, Ellen, but I know you."

Poor Ellen always remained the same, taking more pleasure in doing any one's work than her own, and as she told me, "the soul of her sickened in patching up the clothes of those poor children any more," and, besides, said she: "Everybody else has new clothes, and there's no one on earth quite so proud as a little girl with a new frock."

"But your own trousseau, Ellen," I objected scandalized, because I had a proper sentiment for those things. Ellen was romantic, but seldom sentimental at all.

"Cloth's cloth," she replied briskly, "and goodness knows when I'm to be married and shall need it, and there's one sure thing, they need new best dresses right straight away."

They needed new best dresses and they needed new almost everything else, as Matilda had warned Ellen.

So here was Ellen with her hands full. In the day before the sewing-machine, when every stitch had to be put in by hand and there were no such things as ready-made garments, making clothes for a family was no light undertaking. No wonder, then, that we made our dresses of good stuff, intended to wear; and Ellen had not only to provide for the little Sylvesters garments, but for her own trousseau as well. The young ladies nowadays, who make themselves a few things and order and buy ready-made everything else, do not realize what an undertaking the preparations for a wedding used to be. It sometimes seems to me that there was as much difference in our serious preparation of our clothes and the way that girls prepare now, as there is in the way that we prepared ourselves spiritually. Ellen wrote:—

"The clothes that I am making mean my life, Roger. They are not dresses to me any more. There is one dress I know I shall never be able to put on without feeling my heart beat away the minutes slowly while I waited and waited and waited for your letter. There are some buttonholes made while it seemed as if my heart sang like birds. What do you think I am building with the things I dream of constantly, as I sit with the thought of you and sew on the clothes that I shall wear when we are at last together for always, for thinking is the way that one builds up or tears down the things of the spirit? I think I build rather solidly, and before I can be torn out of this house of my thoughts of you, I shall have to be pulled out in little pieces no bigger than your hand."

She wrote this after she had seen him, for he came for a two days' breathless visit, just as spring was breaking. He came back the bad, little boy, ready to sulk if he was scolded for not coming sooner. This time Ellen had only sweetness for him, no tears; she was so heart-brokenly glad to see him, but she wrote:—

"Where have you gone, Roger, and what's become of that lovely, shining love that we had? The horizon has shrunken for us in a curious way. Where it used to be wider than that of all the world, and the heavens flung full of stars and a splendid wind ramping over everything, our love lives now in a little world full of small hopes and fears, a dwarfed place. I suppose all this means that I wanted to ask you when you were here, 'What's the matter, Roger? What has happened to your love for me?' And I didn't dare to because I knew that you would say, 'Nothing.' I know you would look at me as one who says, 'Am I not here with you now? Don't be a tiresome woman.' When I said to you—and I said it half smiling— 'It's a terrible thing how a man can eat up a woman's life as you do mine, so I am all yours,' you turned away as though you didn't hear me. You made acknowledgment of a word that was only half kind. I write this to you which I would never say to you because if said to you it would be a reproach. I write to you since I have need of my soul talking to yours, and with no reproach in my mind, but to try and understand what it is that has happened. Before, had I shown you my heart that way, you would have caught me to you. Must I be careful not to give you too much of myself, Roger; must I pour myself out to you in small sips,—you who wished to drink of me, as though your thirst for me would never become quenched? It seemed to me that there were as many things to keep silent about while you were here as before we had things to talk about. We were always running into ghosts of the way we used to care, and yet you were so dear to me and sweet to me."

Lovers forever have watched the affections ebb out bit by bit, and have been as powerless to stop the ebbing as the tides of the sea. This causeless change, this heart-breaking wintertime of the affections, is one of the hardest things of all to bear. When people quarrel they can "make up" again, but this slow alteration from life to death comes as relentlessly as age and seems as little in our power to change as age's coming. It has been the anguish of lovers from all time.

All through the coming of spring and summer, Ellen had brooded over this change, wondering if it was her fault, measuring Roger's affection and cherishing every little phrase of love which he put in his letters, every desire to see her, and magnifying them, and stitching all the while her doubts and hopes—hopes a little frayed and tarnished—into her wedding-clothes. There was a time when he promised every week to come, and every week there came a letter instead of Roger. He played fast and loose with her as it suited him, now coming to see her a splendid young prince, now leaving her without word for weeks.

It is an awful and bleeding thing when a woman realizes that the beloved has changed toward her and she doesn't know the reason, and it is still harder to have given more of one's self than has been wanted, and this Ellen did continually. Suffering herself, she wanted to spare Roger suffering.

So she lived along in that hope deferred that maketh the heart sick. Then all word of Roger ceased for a time. She wrote to him as she had always and then she wrote him a letter that she never sent, releasing him.

"Once, when I was a little girl, I thought I was engaged because I thought I was in love, and I spent two years of my life in thinking that my life was dear to this man. I lived in a torment of doubt of what to do rather than hurt him. I could not bear to have any one live this way for me, and least of all you who have been the heart of life to me, and so before this happens to you let us say good-bye to each other as splendidly and gayly as we first met each other. Love does not come at any one's bidding, nor will it stay, and I would blame no one in this world for ceasing to love, least of all the one whom I love. But I could not endure from you a cowardly drifting away from me, I could not bear to see you fear to face bravely a moment of pain, nor could I bear the dishonorable shiftiness with which some men loosen the bonds between themselves and the women whom they have loved."

And under this page, which was written on good notepaper,—a true never-sent letter,—she had written: "Oh! if I had the courage to send this now!"

Then came Roger, triumphant and upstanding, his first pleaded case in his pocket, a splendid young prince again, as prodigal with apologies as he was with love. The miracle happened; they turned back the hands of time for a few days.

"He held me from him, the way he does, at arm's length, and said: 'Ellen, have you doubted me?' What could I say to him? When I had courage enough to say, 'What's been the matter, Roger? Where did you go so I couldn't find you?' he only laughed and said, 'I've been in the devil's own temper.'"

This was the last time she fought against him. From this time on he loosed his careless hand and tightened the clutch of it over her heart until it bled, according to his mood. When she didn't write him for a while he rushed to her, to see that his own was his own, and this was as much as any woman ought to have asked, so he felt. She wrote:—

> "There's one thing I've learned about you, Roger, when first I saw the other Roger, and that was if any one denied you anything, you loved to beg for it. As long as a thing denies itself to you, you must strive for it, and knowing this of you, it is a weapon that I can never use. If I played you as if you were a trout in the stream, played you until I reeled you in to me, tired and gasping, I might have held you in my hand always. Whatever I shall do for you in life, I shall never do anything that shows my love for you more, in that I won't traffic with your love, and keep it for myself by playing a game with you. I make you this present, a real gift, as my aunt once said, and one that you won't know about ever."

So she wrote in the deep bitterness of her heart.

The wedding had been fixed for October and all the time there was one little song that sung itself to her: "When we're married, then I can show him how I really care; when I'm with him, nothing will be hard for me, for it is suspense that kills." For she trusted him as women must, in the face of disloyalty and carelessness.

In the early fall, after a season of silence, when she was too sick at heart even to write, he came. He had a deprecatory air. He came as one asking the favor of something which he ought not to have, and it was characteristic of him, with his intolerance of the disagreeable, that he should break the edge of telling Ellen, so to speak, by telling me first.

He had come to defer the wedding, and his reason for wishing to do so we found out later. I remember how he sat in my kitchen, his heavy, handsome profile silhouetted against the flaming, evening sky, his head swung forward. He lifted his face toward me with a sharp, impatient gesture, looked at me, and asked a question, to me inconceivable.

"Do you think she is going to make an awful fuss?"

CHAPTER XXI

Here my long-cherished resentment toward Roger overflowed. No one could have been with Ellen as I had been without seeing the turmoil in which her spirit lived. She had grown thin and of a certain transparency as do those whose sufferings of the spirit affect their bodies profoundly. I knew there were long times when he didn't write; I knew how she waited for his letters; I knew how seldom he came. I felt, in my wisdom, that she bore from Roger things I would stand from no man. I had learned, step by step with Ellen, that Ellen's life and all her happiness were in careless hands and, in Alec's language, that there was no country of the heart there for her. I looked at Roger with level-eyed disgust.

"Why, Roger," I asked him, "don't you break your engagement now, if that's what you mean to do?"

To my point-blank question, he only stared at me.

"I don't want to break it," he said. "Ellen's just exactly the kind of a woman I want for my wife," he added.

"But in your good time," said I bitterly.

He looked at me with his bold, laughing eyes:

"There's a delight of life with Ellen that I can find with no one else. I know what she is, Roberta, a thousand times more than you. She's the only alive person in the world, but since you put the words in my mouth, 'In my own good time!'" He had completely recovered his good-tempered arrogance.

"I'd never stand from you what Ellen's stood, and I hope she says good-bye to you now," I cried.

It is easy for those not in love to place the limit to love's endurance. It is fortunately not easy to keep these shallow promises to one's self.

I am sorry that so much of what was most unlovely in Roger creeps into my story. At the time I had no patience with him, his undeniable charm and interest offended me as it kept Ellen bound to him. I wanted, as youth always does, people to be all bad or all good, and Roger would be neither of these things. I realize now that, faithful or unfaithful, he kept Ellen's life full of him, nor could she escape his compelling personality. There are many men we should not quarrel with,—men who can so absorb us, like him of the ultra-masculine type, who have everything but pity and understanding of what they themselves haven't felt. They are of all men the most attractive to women and they care the least about the individual. From now on she loved him always with a fear that he was waiting for her with a knife for her back. She wrote:—

"Oh, how much make-believe we have had! I've pretended that I thought it was nice for Roger to work, and he's pretended to me that he wanted to work, but he doesn't want me—that's the real reason. When I wake in the morning, I feel my heart crying within me in the deep heaviness of my spirit before I can remember what's happened, and then I remember that Roger doesn't want me. He doesn't want me and I can't imagine life going on without him. I've always thought to feel unbeloved would be the worst thing that could happen to me. I don't know myself in this beggared person. Life seems so empty for me, and I go shivering up to Alec to warm my cold spirit at the fire of his affection. I look back at the time when I waited for Roger to come back to me, just three little days, and the touch of his hand still warm in mine, and think how happy I was then."

A little later she became more accustomed to the idea and wrote:—

"Roger, I'm ashamed of how I felt, and I'm glad of one thing, that you know nothing about it. Have you seen me as I am, and is that why you no longer care as you did? I've been a cowardly, shivering thing, afraid of your letters even, afraid of what would come next. How can a man love so cowardly a woman? Why should I count and measure love for love, instead of rejoicing with you in your work? It is I that know nothing about love, since I can whine and since I can compare and contrast yesterday with to-day, instead of being glad that you are alive and in the same world with me; and why should I care if, since you want to marry me, you have lost some of the first hot flame, a flame which burned us both? Are all women in life egotists that they can't bear that the eyes of the beloved don't rest on them every moment?"

There was very little use in her trying to hearten herself with brave words, for women know when a part of the life of the man they love belongs to them and when it doesn't. Many of us live for years separated from the man we love, and know that his thoughts turn to us continually, that time and space are a terrible, practical joke played by destiny on mankind. There had been a moment in Ellen's life when, whether he were thinking of her or not, there was no place in his life where she might not go, and now the foundation of a real affection was lacking between them, and that foundation is sincerity. In whatever way she tried to go to him she came upon high walls and barriers of silence, places in his spirit marked "No thoroughfare."

"I know nothing about you, Roger; [she writes] I only know that things are going on that are hostile to me and to our love. I suppose, that you do not tell me what it is shows you do not trust me and that I've grasped too much and asked too much. I fight forever with an unseen adversary. I don't even know if this adversary has a face or if it is a set of circumstances in your life, and I have nothing to fight with but my bleeding love for you, and what good is that to you unless you happen to want it? What thing is so worthless as an undesired love? Yet you made it, Roger, and you are responsible for it. It is like having a child and then finding it troublesome, letting it starve to death, to create a love like mine for you and then kill it. Women who love should never doubt. They should trust and trust in the face of dishonor and in the face of disaster, for distrust carries with it a bitter strength. A woman who trusts utterly is a woman who gives herself utterly, and then, when the blow descends from the blue, it also crushes her utterly, perhaps it may even kill her, but she has had that exalted peace even until the last moment. It's all the difference between having one's beloved brought home dead, who went out smiling, and having him die horribly inch by inch, before one's eyes. It is better to have love killed than to have it tortured to death, and I would rather have had you say, in the midst of our deepest hour together, 'Ellen, I'm going away and I shall never see you again,' than wait as I do for you to tell me it's finished."

This was how Ellen's spirit lived, racked and torn between its grave fears and its momentary and joyful hopes, while the day was passed in a thousand details of a house humming with children. As Ellen said herself, "The outer side of her life was living in sunshine and the inner side in darkness and doubt." In town people said Ellen was working too hard over Mr. Sylvester's brood, for she seemed at that time so frail that through the transparent shell of her one could see her spirit burning.

None of the family suspected that there was any misunderstanding between them, for Roger had a very kindly generosity. He was a man prodigal in the small acts of kindness, and was forever sending things for the children and for Mrs. Sylvester, whom he treated like an elder sister, teasing her and loving her. Miss Grant was the only one who had had occasional misgivings, and I learned from my grandmother that Roger's family were not satisfied with his "goings on," and that while he was being a success, his mother was worried over him, which made my grandmother remark:—

"I wish that young man had fallen from his horse and broken his neck before ever he set eyes on Ellen Payne. Old women like us forget that young creatures die of a broken heart now and again, and if they could only die! The best friend I ever had, Roberta, had all the youth and love killed in her and went on living like a dry, little automaton of a woman, and is living yet. Instead of the things she might have had,—children and a husband and a home,—she has just her own dried-up body, which is like a little birch tree struck by lightning; and the thing she thinks of most in life is the noise that the sparrows make in her elm trees."

But I could not fear that a fate like that awaited my Ellen, for my memory of her then is a lovely frail thing, with a hand forever held out to Prudentia and Flavilla.

Prudentia when crossed stopped, as was her custom, to pray. She prayed in season and out of season and for everything, and it was against her father's principles to stop her.

"How stop a child communing with her Maker?" he would argue, to which Ellen would reply with spirit: —

"She's only communing with her own selfishness when she says: 'Oh! God, send the boys home so Ellen can tell me a story.'"

For several of Alec's youngsters hung around the old Scudder place a great deal, and accompanied Ellen on her walks, as though Alec had left her, in those boys, a bit of his protecting spirit.

CHAPTER XXII

Various important things happened that winter. The first was a deep surprise to all of Alec's friends. He became engaged to his landlady's daughter in the town where he went to college.

"How can you?" I asked him, "caring for Ellen?"

"Well, you see," he explained, "it's all over, isn't it, forever? No matter what happens, Ellen is Roger's, and why should I hang around and bay the moon? Elizabeth knows all about Ellen."

"I don't see how you can," I repeated.

And then he said:—

"Roberta, it seems a wonderful thing to me that any one should care for me. How can I hurt a love that has been given to me? I care for her in a different way from Ellen and there is all truth between us." Then he laughed. "It's a funny thing; Roger loves no one, Ellen loves Roger, I love Ellen, and Elizabeth cares for me. By doing this I'm making the tangle less."

That is all he would tell me at the time, but, being romantic then and still romantic, I have always thought that his chivalry and compassion had been skillfully played upon.

With a touching belief in the generosity of woman that is possible only in extreme youth, Alec effected a meeting between Elizabeth and Ellen at which I was present. All three of us were painfully polite and well behaved. Our cordiality was touching as we played to our dear Alec as audience. "But," said Ellen to me afterwards, "isn't it dreadful! why couldn't he have chosen any one else! She's sweet, of course; but think, Roberta, of that doll-faced thing as Alec's wife." While Elizabeth is reported to have said that on beholding Ellen she could hardly keep herself from exclaiming aloud, "Why, is that Ellen Payne!"

It was in midwinter that Mrs. Byington asked Ellen to visit her. She had often asked Ellen before, but there had been various reasons; Roger always preferred to spend the time with Ellen in the country. It seemed to me that in the days of her preparation it was like seeing a person come back to life. She has written:—

"I've been so homesick for you, Roger, that I felt like those people who die of homesickness in a far-off country. I feel as though I had been put away in a place where there was no air to breathe, and now I am to be let out into the sunlight once more, since you want me to come to you."

Roger came back with her, but during the week she was away there was no entry at all. The visit was a time of confusion and excitement. Mrs. Byington gave her three beautiful frocks, more beautiful than anything she had ever seen, and it seemed to Ellen that she had met the whole city of Boston, and that she had been drowned in compliments. They seemed to her to have only just learned of her engagement, and she felt the weight of their curious eyes upon her, and realized that they turned from compliments to gossip, and Mrs. Byington, in the mean time, scarcely concealed her relief at Ellen's presence and her pleasure at the impression Ellen had made. Miss Sarah told these things to my grandmother, having accompanied Ellen.

Ellen made one friend, a girl younger than herself, a cousin of Roger's, who unconsciously played a part, since she put in Ellen's hands the answer to so many riddles, the uncertainties that so tortured her.

"Now I know all the things that tortured me so," she wrote. "I felt that I was in Boston for some definite purpose that I didn't know about, and the reason Katherine showed me, as though she had flung out a careless hand and pulled back a curtain, and I felt as though I had listened at Roger's door. 'Aunt Lydia was glad enough to have you come,' said she. 'Of course, we in the family have known of Roger's engagement, even if he hasn't talked about it outside, but since his quarrel with Mary Leckie, he's been eager enough too.' And her little careless words gave me a picture of all the things I didn't know, but that I had felt, and as if to make it sure it seemed that Mrs. Byington apologized to me when she said: 'Roger is making great strides at his profession; it is a compensation for many things to know that the man one loves is a man of great attainment.' It is as though my heart had been dried up suddenly. I look back at the time when I could cry as a time of happiness. If he should love some one more than me, how could I blame him, but he has used me as a pawn in the game, to hurt some one he's been unkind to, perhaps some one who loved him, too. What attainment of his can wipe out this cruelty? I saw the little look of triumph on his face when he saw his friends approved of me. Now what hope have I or where can I turn in this world? I have just one good little word to cling to—he said to me wistfully, 'Oh! Ellen, why wouldn't you run away with me?' They say love is blind, but no man knows or excuses a man so little as the woman who loves him."

She had not seen him alone when she wrote this, as Miss Grant accompanied them home. It was on Saturday afternoon, and they went walking on the road to meet Alec, that Ellen learned her own heart. Roger was in a dangerous mood, kind on the surface, but underneath a mood that said: "Take me or leave me; I am as I am." Perhaps he regretted burning his bridges behind him; perhaps he chafed at the restraint of the inevitable marriage. For once he was ready to draw the hidden things to the surface. Ellen wrote:—

"I know now who I am, and I know that I have no pride in the world and that there's no place where I stop in my love for Roger; no matter what he does to me, I cannot leave him; no matter what happens, I ask only to be with him. We started out across the mountain. It was slushy underfoot and the cold, damp air whining up from the river. All the world looked sullen, and a sad little moon peered through a hole in the clouds. I felt inside as sad and cold as the world seemed. Roger walked along, his head thrown forward, looking into the dusk the way he looked at his mother. At last he said: 'Did you have a good time in Boston, Ellen?' And I knew he was questioning me as to what I had seen, throwing the door open on everything; and I had gone out with him, meaning to tell him what I thought and stand and fall by that. I said to myself a hundred times to-day, 'There are better things in this world than happiness,' but at his menacing voice I could say nothing. I looked down into the abyss of my need of him and there was no bottom to it. I felt that at a word from me he would quarrel with me, perhaps fling me away from him, and I didn't dare say anything. After a long silence he said: 'You look dispirited, Ellen; you're never happy, are you, unless some one is telling you that you're the Rose of the World?' Tears burned behind my eyes, but I turned his challenge into a joke. In that moment I had seen what life would mean without him, and I saw it wouldn't be life, that I am his at his own price—no matter what I must do, no matter what I must suffer, if he gives me faith or unfaith. I thought I had pride, but I know now that I ask for nothing but to stay near him at his own terms. I know there is nothing I would not do to keep him by my side, that the only thing intolerable to me is that he should leave me. There's no little pride or self-respect left for me to wrap myself in any more. I walked beside him fighting back the tears, and it was like a deliverance to me when Alec came striding toward me, his head up, and his hair blowing in the wind, and I could blot out myself for a minute. When we got home, the three children were in the cold hall. Matilda and Flavilla were trying to make Prudentia come in, and Prudentia was praying, as she had been for half an hour, that I would come home. My little mother met me very shame-faced and said, 'Dearest, see what I've found,' and it was an enormous bag of holey stockings that she had put away to mend as a surprise for me, and had forgotten, and all the little details of life wrapped around me sweetly, but it's hard to have every one good to me but the one whom I love."

Love has its base places and its hideous slaveries of the spirit, but yet there is a certain comfort in utter abandonment. Ellen was like a man who has feared bankruptcy and who breathes again when he has at last actually failed; she had nothing to lose any more in her own spirit. She might lose Roger, but no other thing, for she now asked for nothing for herself. She had reached the lowest grade where one's soul may live, when she knows there is nothing that one wouldn't suffer at the hands of the beloved. Pride comes first—a blessed relief—between most women and such pain; but many women know something of the shame akin to it when they sacrifice their sincerity and their sense of truth rather than run the risk of a frown from the man they love.

The whole event had been one of unspeakable defeat and horror to Ellen; all that was fair and sweet in life to her turned black. There was no explaining away or excusing what Roger had done; she was too fair-minded to try. She saw the act in all its smallness, but it didn't affect her want of him. During the next dark months she had all the pain of one who has been utterly abandoned by her lover, and she suffered, too, from jealousy and was ashamed of her suffering. Because she had told herself the truth about herself always, she had not even the disillusion that she was playing a fine and noble part. She only knew that it was no virtue of hers, but just a necessity for her to continue to spend herself endlessly for Roger. Her body, too, suffered pitifully, and she seemed to me to do nothing but wait for the meager words that Roger sent her.

Then happened in her heart that which I now know is the climax of the whole story. I knew nothing of it except that I knew that at a certain time Ellen grew happier.

She stopped waiting and became again master of her own soul, and the light of her spirit shone high again. She told me nothing, for things like this one cannot tell to another person. How can we tell another person of the rebirth of one's own soul?

> "I don't know how to tell what has happened to me, [wrote Ellen,] but I know that I have come to the other side of suffering. I know it is as though I had been sitting at the bottom of a dark well, and suddenly, in the blackness of the sky above me, I saw a star and climbed out toward it. I

know I shall lose this vision and go stumbling on, but sometimes it will come back to me; and I shall always have the memory of it and never again can I be in the muddy darkness in which my spirit has lived. I sat awake all night thinking of Roger in a flooding tenderness of love and understanding, and I realized that in all this time I've only just been learning the first painful paths on the road of love. Whatever one gives sorrowfully isn't love, nor does love fear; it asks only to understand more and more. As long as one has fear, one thinks of one's self; as long as one is sad, one thinks of one's self. Until one has learned not to say, 'Give, give,' one doesn't know the meaning of love. So many sins are committed in the name of love continually and I will commit no more. 'I love you' has been a reason even for killing the ones whom we love, but for this one night I have had a vision of something that transcends love of self. Let me give and let me understand. Love must be either an equal exchange between equals or else a complete giving by one person, so let my giving be complete."

So it was that from a woman ashamed of her own abasement, Ellen walked forth with head up, meeting the difficulties that life put to her and turning them into sweetness. Roger felt this change in her. Lately all intercourse between them had been, on Ellen's side, a silent questioning, and on his side, silent anger at her questioning; and the whole situation scarcely less strained than had they talked to each other. After having gone through the painful Calvary of love, the pain of waiting and the pain of doubt, and of trust misplaced and of jealousy, she had come through to the other side of grief.

Her high mood had made her see life so truly that an event which shocked the rest of us did not touch her, since she saw it in its true relation to Roger's life, even though it again put off her wedding, violently and cataclysmally.

He came during the winter occasionally, looking rather haggard and gaunt and ill at ease with life, and he rested himself more and more on her breast as if trying further and further and with deeper confidence this unspeakable affection of hers.

Miss Sarah brought the news to our house, and she was agitated as I never have seen her.

"You may as well stay, Roberta," she said, "because, after all, it may be better that you shall tell Ellen. No," she contradicted herself, "no one shall carry my burdens for me."

"What's happened to Roger?" my grandmother asked; and I sat silent and trembling, pictures of a dead Roger in my mind.

"Roger's father has turned him off; he's been mixed up in some disgraceful gambling scrape. He's been very wild this winter, poor Lydia writes me,—poor heart-broken woman. He escaped actual arrest only through his father's influence."

Little by little the whole series of events were made clear before my horrified young eyes. Country New England in those days was a place of rigid morals, nor were young girls taught to condone the frailties of men, and gambling at that time had a guilty and glittering sound. All our feelings, I think, were, how fortunate it should have occurred before Ellen's wedding. When Miss Sarah told her, she said:—

"I know, he's written me already," but she didn't add, "And I've written him to come to me." She wrote:—

> "When I got his letter telling me what had happened and releasing me, it seemed to me as if all the smouldering love in me for him burst into flame, and now, in the moment when every one's turned on him, I am triumphantly and gladly his more than ever I've been. I feel as if I could stretch out my arms to him in the darkness and shield him from all harm and trouble. I feel as if I had been talking with him face to face, and that all this had burned away all those things that have been between us all this time. And he turned to me at this time with 'I suppose you, too, Ellen, will want no more of me, but I wish, Ellen, I could say good-bye to you myself instead of writing it— you've been so true, Ellen.'"

So in the spring, two years after she first met Roger, Ellen went to Oscar's Leap to await his coming. She loved the gallant bearing of him, for he came no broken penitent. He was no coward before the challenge of life; he loved the difficult and had a lovely joy in such battles.

"They kicked me out, Ellen," he told her, "and I've kicked them all out. Now it's me with my own two hands and my own two feet and you in the world. Why didn't you tell me to do this before?" He loved the feeling he had of foot-looseness. He needed just one person to hold a hand out to him in the general wreckage of life, and his own woman had done this for him. When he got her letter, it seemed to him as though he had fallen to the earth only to spring up strong again.

This time Ellen's whole family was against her, even to Mr. Sylvester, whose gentle nature always distrusted Roger. He had feared him from the first, having that gift of judgment of character that gentle and simple people often have. Ellen writes:—

"We had a fine scene, like that in a novel, at our house. Mr. Sylvester forbade Roger the house, and I flung myself in Roger's arms and said that I would never leave him. Mother cried, and I could hear the children breathing at the keyhole and Prudentia praying in the hall. I suppose I should take it more seriously. I am sorry to be at odds with them, but what difference does it make to me, after all? I am glad just that Roger is back. If I could go with him now out into the world, I would put my hand in his and go, but the last thing he needs at this moment is a wife, and the first thing of all he needs is me. Now all my days of waiting have been paid for, now all my nights of doubt. If after this he should turn from me and love me no more, I should have had this and it would have paid for everything in my life. I can't take Mr. Sylvester's and my mother's attitude seriously, because I know, as if I could read the future, that Roger will go out in the world and come back and be forgiven. I am wrong to be almost glad that it has happened, but it has made it possible for me to show him my heart, my poor bleeding heart, that has been silent for so long."

Roger found work in a neighboring village and they met at the house of Ellen's old friend, the peddler, or he took Ellen with him. During this time Roger flung from him again all of his life. He was one whom the confessional would have served well, for he could purge himself from all blame by telling everything and by passing to the innocent the burden of all his weaknesses. Now that life made some demand on him, the best of him shone out.

There was, to be sure, the making of a fine family scandal when it was discovered that Ellen was meeting Roger, but Ellen refused to quarrel; she refused to defend herself or do anything but laugh; and when I, rather scandalized at the lightness with which she took this whole situation, pointed out that her aunt was sulking and that her mother and Mr. Sylvester were sad, she replied with levity: "They'll get over it." During the long winter of silence and of forging her spirit into this flaming thing it now was, she had learned that lesson which is so difficult for youth, and that is that all things pass and that to-morrow brings peace to the bruised heart.

Her prophecy concerning Roger came to pass. After the weeks spent with her he went West, made friends with a friend of his father,—who had a lighter attitude toward Roger's frailties, having had no opportunity to be tired out by them,—did well in pleading some spectacular cases, and came back, not the prodigal son, but triumphantly and gladly; then after his year of self-denial he plunged deeply into all sorts of amusements.

CHAPTER XXIII

Ellen, during his absence, had kept closer and closer to her high mood. She knew that certain sorts of happiness were not for her with Roger, and that certain things he did and his moments of neglect and forgetfulness no longer wounded her to death. A month before her marriage she went to Boston again to buy her best things. Mrs. Sylvester had had a small legacy left her, and insisted that it must go to Ellen's trousseau. I accompanied Mrs. Sylvester and Ellen. Roger was frankly relieved in his mind to have Ellen in Boston and the day of his wedding at last in sight.

"There was never a man," he told me, "looked forward to his wedding with greater eagerness. I'm through with philandering, Roberta. No one knows more than I what Ellen has stood for my sake."

I knew he was referring to a mild flirtation gossip concerning him which had come to Ellen and to me.

It seemed as if now nothing could come in their way and as if all was clear before them. Almost every detail was provided for when Ellen's prayer that she had prayed day by day and day by day—"Give me understanding and insight"—received its supreme answer.

It was Roger's temperament, and Ellen understood this, to fill the vacant places in his life with small love-affairs. At first she had suffered a certain jealousy and afterwards humiliation, and then dismissed it all as negligible, never thinking of it, as was natural, from the other woman's point of view. This last vague affair had been with a young girl visiting from the South, who hadn't known Roger was engaged, as he supposed she had. I noticed in the different places where we went a little, frail figure with a pretty, strained face, with eyes continually and irritatingly on Roger. His mother had said of him, "He's not one who kisses and tells, but one who kisses and runs"; and he was avoiding her with his instinctive avoidance of the disagreeable. She was a foolish, suffering girl, like Ellen without pride, and even lacking the guard of Ellen's reserve, haunting what she had thought had been her love for the balm of a single word which, though she had lost him, would make his memory sweet to her.

We were at a great party given by one of Roger's relatives, in Ellen's honor, two dazzled, little country Cinderellas, and for a moment had drawn ourselves apart to a recess of the big hall, and we saw Roger looking for us. The young girl hurrying across ran almost into his arms, and as they stood she cried out, in a little flowing voice, "Roger." His face went white with anger and set itself into the lines that since then have been known as "his sentencing face." He didn't speak, but looked at her with quiet, cruel, and scornful eyes. There was silence between them, and she tortured the long white gloves that she held in her nervous hands, looking so frail that a breath might have blown her away.

"I've been trying to speak to you."

"I think we said all that was necessary before," he told her with the same cold, white scorn. He had been stopped in his search for what he wanted, and here was being made a scene that he had tried to avoid.

"I've been trying not to speak to you," he said very quietly, "because I had nothing to say to you that could please you."

Then tormented out of herself, she cried out:

"Roger, was there no reality of any friendship between us? Were you engaged all the time that I've known you?"

"There's been nothing between us. What should there be? Just a moonshine of words," he answered her. "I've been engaged three years. Do you wish anything else?"

She didn't answer, but went away, a lonely, little, fragile figure, shivering as though struck with a great cold. He had had no moment of compassion; his instinct had been to crush her with as little pity as he would an annoying fly. In his ruthlessness he took even the past from her, not even leaving her the shadow of her romance for comfort. Ellen and I had both seen her wilt before him and the light in her eyes go out, and I felt Ellen's hand shaking in mine as the girl had shivered, and she whispered in my ear:—

"There, but for the grace of God, goes Ellen Payne."

Here was her prayer granted and understanding was given her. The final tragedy is not to be unloved, but to find out that one has loved nothing;—that within the shell of the body there is nothing to which we can give ourselves;—to have been cursed with the love of the shallow-hearted; and there is a deep torment, beyond the loss of death, which goes with the unknitting of two souls knit close together, strand by strand. Ellen could stand any cruelty that he gave to her and condone it, but she shivered back from this relentlessness that she had seen in Roger. As he came to her she said to him:—

"I heard you, Roger."

His face was still set in anger.

"I gave her no cause," he exclaimed angrily, "nothing but a little moonshine talk. When we're married I shan't be subjected to things like that."

"We're not going to be married," said Ellen.

CHAPTER XXIV

During all my life long I have occasionally had, in times of stress, a recurrence of the spiritual nausea which I felt that night. When we drove home in the closed carriage Mrs. Sylvester was prattling like a girl about the beautiful party. Indeed, she had enjoyed the outward circumstance of things almost more than Ellen and myself, and Roger, making light talk with her, sat next to Ellen,—light talk that had its undercurrent of meaning that Ellen and I understood. The cab lurched noisily over the cobblestones, with which all Boston was paved in those days, so that Roger and Mrs. Sylvester had to raise their voices above the din. It was raining, and the yellow flare of the street-corner lamps was reflected in pools of eddying light from the damp pavements.

It seemed to me that we went on and on forever in this torment of noise and talk, and the smell of the wet spring night conflicted with the smell of the stuffy upholstery, and I suffered as though I was witnessing the physical pain of a tortured child. It seemed to me that the torment of the ceaseless, agonizing prattle of Ellen's little mother, accompanied by the drunken lurch of the lumbering cab, would never stop, for all the time I knew that Ellen's heart was breaking, and that the only thing that life could give her at that moment was darkness and rest. I knew this was the end as far as she and Roger were concerned.

We had our room together, and I felt like a stranger in a house of mourning. I knew that there was no comfort that I could give her at all. She hadn't even tears with which to refresh herself, and all she said to me was: "Roberta, I've been stripped bare of leaves to-night." This was a true enough picture of her. She had been a blooming flower, and now it was as if the frost of some inexorable and unseen winter had touched her and she was bare of leaves and blossoms.

I suppose I was the only one among all those who loved her who did not urge Ellen to reflect on her decision. There was so little to tell when it came to it. Ellen's reason was so little one of the usual causes for which an engagement may be dissolved, with the approval of a girl's elders. Here was Ellen who had stood by Roger gayly, without even, apparently, a proper understanding of his dissipation; who had endured from him neglect, who had learned to school herself so that she was able to ignore his temperamental interests in other women; she, who had been without any end in her affections, gave the appearance to the outside world of having suddenly, for no reason, come to an end of her love.

In our town there was scant belief that Ellen had jilted Roger. Why do such a thing? "Aren't they all as poor as church mice, and isn't Roger as likely a young man as one would wish to see?" They clamored around me inquisitively.

There is no time when the human race shows itself in such beauty and in such heartless sordidness as in the time of grief. Then it is that the world we know turns strange faces upon us, and mean, low-lived men will show the gentle chivalry that one would expect only of angels, and delicate women, of chaste and gracious lives, will develop, before one's eyes, hideous and ghoulish curiosity. Any one who has been through the death of those whom they love knows this, and still more it is true in the other disasters of life, where there is no ceremonial of grief. Death has dignity. Its august finality stops many a wagging tongue and many an unkind word. But oh, the other griefs of the spirit! One is shielded by no mourning; there is no protecting tradition to fold its arms about one; and one's poor, shivering soul is left naked on the highway, afraid of the heartless curiosity of prying eyes.

The curious world has no mercy for a girl jilted by her lover. There is no sanctity to all this suffering, no privacy allowable, not a day's respite from the inquisitive natures and prattling tongues. One must count one's self very fortunate if one is allowed to care for the most bleeding of one's wounds with a certain degree of decent privacy. And in our little town privacy was what was impossible for Ellen. I was for a while the center of the storm, for, to Roger, Ellen had been inexplicable; he had not been able to believe what had happened and came storming down after us.

"I can't see him," Ellen told me. "There's no place anywhere in him to explain anything. You'll see when you try and talk to him."

I begged her, out of kindness, to see him once because he was

terribly torn by what had happened. He told me that the sure
foundations of life had rocked under his feet, and when I repeated
this to Ellen, she shook her head.

"It's not that,—he can't bear that what's been so his creature
should defy him. He's never had life say no to him before." She said
this without bitterness, and more as an older woman might of a boy
she has brought up.

"Why won't you see him," I pleaded with her, "just for one
moment?"

"I don't dare to," she told me. "Every habit I have says yes to
him; every strand of my body cries out to him; it's as if he had
never been and I had died; and yet our bodies go on living and
caring for each other. He doesn't need me any more than he needs
any one else. He needs no person, Roberta. Love and
encouragement and companionship: the world is full of it for him.
Yet I need him and shall need him always, to the end of my days."

Often it is that in the disintegration of a deep and long-lived
affection, it is the instinct of the body to shiver away first, before the
mind knows what has happened, but it is more dangerous when, in
the full splendor of love, the blow has fallen and instinct still
clamors for the beloved's companionship.

But she wasn't to be spared seeing him. They met by chance
upon the street. I was with Ellen, and he began at once babbling
forth the excuses he had said over and over to me. Because Ellen
said there was no place in him to tell him what it was all about, he
persisted in thinking that she had been outraged by his trifling
again, with their affection, at the eleventh hour.

At last he went away, but he had the satisfaction of feeling that
he had played the noble part. In the light of Ellen's actions, what he
considered his own small unfaiths, appeared as nothing.

> "Now you are gone [she wrote] I would call you back
> if I could, and I have to remember and say to myself that
> there is no one to call back. There is nothing in you that
> would hear the things that I wish to say to you, and yet
> you go on living and yet I must love you; and yet, forever
> and ever in the night, my heart goes out to you; and yet,

when I walk along, I feel the touch of your hand, as though it were placed in mine. But the you that meant life to me never was, or died, perhaps, with your boyhood. He was there a little while and smiled at me, and all the time the real you was growing large and strong and killing that other whom I loved. But I have bound my life up in you, so what can I do, and where will I find comfort? I can have scarcely the comfort of a memory, for I have loved only a ghost in you. I envy those sad and haggard girls who have been deserted by their lovers. I envy wives who have been left with little children to care for, for they, at least, have had reality; they have been able to give all of themselves, and what they have known has been real. I wonder if I shall always have to bleed for you, drop by drop, and that while I bleed, my strength also goes? Everything talks to me of you. My hand stretches out for a pen and I must write to you, though you aren't, and yet you are dearer to me than all the world besides. Where did the sweet soul of you go that I loved so well, and how can I live in a world where such things happen? I go out upon the street and hear people walking past and children playing and think with surprise, 'Why, there are happy people in the world!'"

CHAPTER XXV

If the world has little pity for a jilted girl, how shall it have much understanding for any one who suffers after having voluntarily sent her lover away, especially when it was her obvious duty to her family to marry? So her world was not very kind to Ellen at a moment when she most needed their kindness. We do not often understand the sicknesses of the spirit; now we mete out to them the criminal indulgence that a foolish woman does to a wayward child, and now we treat them with bruising harshness.

During the summer matters were not so bad, because every one rather expected that Ellen would come to herself. My grandmother used to question me seriously if I were encouraging Ellen.

Even Mr. and Mrs. Sylvester, most unworldly people,—more unworldly, I think, than any one I have ever known,—had seen the children "enjoying advantages" through Ellen, for Ellen and Roger had planned a thousand things.

Matilda had wept openly when Ellen had returned, and said:—

"Oh, Ellen, Ellen! Now that you're not going to be married, I suppose I shall never visit you and study music in Boston, and, Ellen, I had so make-believed it in my heart."

During the summer there was little written in her journal except letters to Roger, which stopped abruptly with her determination to get over the aching want which she had for him. With the coming of winter there settled down over Ellen a limitless depression. She was very gentle, but she seemed lost in a mist of sadness. I cannot describe to what extent her spirit was dimmed. It seemed as though a strange, withering age had crept over her before her time. People noticed it, and word went abroad that Ellen Payne was "in a decline," which was a word for almost everything that ailed one in those days, short of a broken leg. I remember her walking around at that time with poses of a very tired child, for all the hollow under her eyes and the troubled lines in her forehead. She would let her arms swing before her like a little girl that had outgrown her strength, and throw herself down into chairs as though she had held herself on her feet to the utmost limits of her endurance.

I ventured to ask her at last: "What's the matter, Ellen?" For we had avoided, by common consent, talking of anything that might be wounding, and had put the past out of sight.

She looked at me with eyes that had the hurt look of a little girl.

"I'll tell you what's the matter," she told me in answer. "I know well enough what's the matter. There's no meaning to life any more at all. The world goes on over there"—she waved her hand ever so slightly—"and I'm here on the outside, and what they do doesn't mean anything at all, Roberta. If life goes on like this, maybe I'll be lucky enough to die, and the worst of it is that the hope of dying is keeping me alive. I am afraid, Roberta, that when one has anything to live for, even if it's dying, that one keeps on living. What it really means," she added, "is that I've lost God, for I can't pray any more."

Since then I've known a great many women in mortal pain, and I truly believe that it is the nearness of death that keeps many a suffering soul alive. They are forever heartening themselves by looking through the black, mysterious door, where there is an end to pain and where one need not stay famished any more at life's feast. Death walks consolingly so close; death is so easy and calls compassionately to these forsaken ones, saying, "Out here is rest— so near; if it gets much worse, you can come to me." Wherever one looks there is the consoling possibility of death, and since death is so near and so easy, people, who have forgotten for a while the reason for living, go on just the same. For who, in the winter of the spirit, can again believe in spring?

At this time even the children seemed to turn away from Ellen and give her nothing. She had always meant laughter and gayety and the heightening of the lives of all of us around her, and Alec and I were the only two who remained faithful to her in this moment of desolation, because the others did not see Ellen in this docile, lifeless soul, who went around still called by the name of Ellen Payne; and this withdrawal of human sympathy was as unconscious as it was wounding. My sweet old grandmother, who had loved Ellen so, combined with old Mrs. Butler, whose hair

Ellen had done for years,—since Alec had grown up,—would nod
their heads together and say that Ellen Payne ought to stop those
mopish ways and use more backbone.

That winter Ellen's mother was ailing and coughed badly also,
and for the first time in her life was a little querulous and
complaining. I ignored as much as I could Ellen's ill feelings, as she
wished me to do, but I remember this tragic winter well. There
were a very few entries in her journal, but not in this or in any other
crisis of her life had she failed to clarify her mind by the written
word. I find this:—

> "I try as hard as I can to attach myself to the duties
> that crowd around me. Sometimes it just seems to me that
> I am going to succeed in being interested and then I am
> not. I think it must be like this in those strange northern
> countries, where the glow of dawn comes on the horizon,
> and, starved for light, one says, 'Here is the dawn'; and
> even as one speaks the light pales and the dreadful
> twilight thickens around one."

Towards spring—one of those soppy, wet springs, when it
seems as though the green would never come—I could stand the
silence no longer, and some word or look of hers that betrayed to
me the desolate abasement of her spirit made me cry out:—

"Ellen, isn't there anything on earth that you want?"

"I think I would like to see Alec," she answered.

It seemed to me a foolish wish, for Alec was in his first school
and far away, and his visits to us had been spasmodic and brief,
and shared, of course, with Elizabeth Greenough, though during
the summer he had been home and spent a good deal of time with
Ellen, and she had accepted his kindness as she always had, very
much as the air one breathes, or as she accepted my friendship—as
one of the certain things among the deep uncertainties of life.

I wrote to Alec what Ellen had said, without a hope in the
world that he could come. It seemed the sort of thing that only love
accomplishes, and he had seemed to me perfectly contented with
his engagement, making his visits to the home of his young lady

with the regularity of a lover, or of a clock. But almost sooner than seemed possible he came. When Ellen saw him tears came to her eyes. For it is just at these moments, when one is thirsting for help and sympathy, that we seem to lose the way to the hearts of others, and this is natural enough, for there is a terrible egotism in certain phases of grief. The eyes of the spirit are turned inward and we cease to give, and after a while, as with Ellen, grief becomes a habit and we slip along smoothly enough in the deepening and dolorous grooves of sorrow. It is easier to do this where the outside life is monotonous, and to us, in our little town, our own point of view and our own spirits furnished whatever diversity there was. One day went along after another and one never met a new face on the street, and it was with a true instinct for help that Ellen cried out:—

"I envy men who can go out in the world and forget. It must be easier to forget among those who have never seen your face or ever heard what has happened to you, and here everything brings me back to the thoughts that I try in so futile a fashion to put out of my mind."

Alec's unexpected arrival had been the only thing that had happened through the long winter and spring. I waited with anxiety for the end of their interview.

"Well," I asked Alec, "how did you find her?"

And he answered:—

"She just wants to know how one manages to live when the meaning of life is dead and I told her that that wasn't what she needed, but that she needed to go and search for the meaning of life, and you know, Roberta, a person who really seeks for that can always find it. I've a plan that I'm going to try. Ellen has promised to do everything I tell her, and keep her to it, even if it seems childish to you."

A day or two after Alec left, there knocked at the Sylvesters' back door a sturdy boy of twelve; a shock of wild black hair blew across his forehead, and funny, humorous blue eyes gleamed under straight black brows. For the rest, he was freckled past belief. As Ellen opened the door for him, he choked in a spasm of embarrassment, then the words came, with a rush. He had a deep voice for his age.

"I've come to git Ellen Payne," he boomed.

When Ellen, who had opened the door for him, said:—

"Why, I'm Ellen Payne and what do you want?" he flushed furiously and muttered:—

"He said you was a girl."

"Well," responded Ellen, with more briskness than she had shown for some time, "I'm a girl."

"No," replied the boy, "you're a grown-up woman, tall 's ever you'll be."

"Did you say you had come to get me?" suggested Ellen.

"He said you was to come with me."

"What are we going to do?" asked Ellen.

"Git mayflowers in a place you don't know," said the boy.

"There's no such place," said Ellen. "I know every cranny of this place in my sleep."

"Well, I know it as if I'd made it," retorted the boy.

By the time Ellen came back ready to walk, a wave of shyness engulfed the boy; he was as uncommunicative as the Pyramids. He was deeply embarrassed by his companion, but he forgot now and then enough to go ahead, shouting his joy at the return of spring, and then his gayety would fall as a flag at half-mast when he saw Ellen after him. She came home wet and very tired, to listen to the prophecy of her Aunt Sarah that "no good would come of this weltering around in the wet, and that it was just like one of Alec's unpractical thoughts."

While Miss Sarah loved Alec, his character annoyed her, winding as it did around a devious road and springing upon you new view-points, as a supposedly quiet road might discover unexpected and romantic vistas of country. Especially his attitude toward the boys was annoying to those who found difficulty in having wood-piles replenished and the "chores" done.

"You'd think boys were something," my grandmother used to explain with some heat, "besides trying, rascally, little scallywags; but the older you grow, Roberta, the more you'll find truth in what I say, and that is, that boys were put in this world by the Lord for women to exercise their patience over."

Tyke Bascom didn't come again for two days. This time Ellen

penetrated through the shyness enough to find that he was a boy who lived over the mountain-road in a little clearing, called Foster's Corners, which had a sawmill and four houses.

"That's a long ways," said Ellen.

"Not so long when you're used to it," he replied. "It might be long for a woman."

In his walks over the mountain, Alec had always stopped at the house and, being fatal to small boys, Tyke had enrolled in the company of Alec's friends. All that Tyke knew, it turned out, he had been taught by Alec, as he sat there resting on his way home.

For the next two weeks Tyke Bascom came for Ellen, but irregularly. Sometimes he would come each day, for two or three days, and once three days went past, three days when Ellen watched for him. It had been a long time since she had been out in the open air; it had been a long time since she had gone back to the places she had known as a little girl, when she was in that deep and almost mystic communion with all life and growth around her, and when the mountain and the river, and the small mountain streams were like personalities to her. Only the very pure in heart and children have this intimate sense of oneness with the world, and Ellen and Alec had lain for hours, under cover, and watched to see a fox sneak past. They knew a marsh where the blue heron lived, and when she was little, Ellen had talked about the birds, squirrels, and chipmunks as intimately as though they were people.

Now all this forgotten lore came back to her from out-of-the-way places in her mind. When I was a girl, it was only too easy for people to forget such things, for in my day, no sooner did one grow up than the customs of young ladyhood demanded that one should spend most of one's time in the house. Even skating was denied women, and Ellen's love of the outdoors met with a steady stream of disapproval from every one, including Roger. The only people who had not frowned on her were her mother and Mr. Sylvester, who held the heretical theory that it was good even for a woman to know the works of the Lord, even though a close and intimate knowledge was bad for smoothness of hair and neatness of frock.

More than that, there was a desire awakened in Ellen's mind,

of conquering this wild and morose child, who had given his heart
so unreservedly to Alec.

She asked him,—

"Do you like going out with me, Tyke?"

"No 'm," he said, "not especially."

"But"—she told him—"you don't need to come if you don't
want to."

He flushed all over and said, "I didn't mean that. Don't you
see, Alec told me to, so I don't mind at all, 'cause it's for him."

"Now I realize," she wrote, "that whenever I've sat down
anywhere children have always come around me. Until the last
year or two I've known all the little boys; there's never been a time
when some of Alec's youngsters haven't been perched in our yard,
and now comes along this boy who takes me out with him as he
would carry a package for Alec."

There was nothing for it, she must make him her own. I think it
was the first desire she had had in a year's time, except the desire
for the ultimate peace. She wooed him first out of his shyness, and
as I would see them talking together I would see all the mannerisms
of the Ellen I had known, of whom Aunt Sarah said, "She seemed
about to burst into flame." All her forgotten shy guiles that had led
her before into the inaccessible hearts of boys woke up one by one. I
don't know how far she went back on the road to childhood, in
these rambles, or how much she remembered of the golden time
when Alec and she played truant together by the hills and brooks.

One day Tyke appeared with this command:

"You got to come up to my house, he says; ma needs help,
she's sick. He sent you this."

He gave her a note from Alec which read:—

"Dear Ellen: It was always easier for you to do housework out
of your house than in."

That was all.

"Ma's sick; she's got a new baby."

So every day Ellen trudged over the mountain-road and back.
No sooner was Mrs. Bascom beginning to be up and around again,
and Ellen still going to see her and the baby, than Mrs. Sylvester

hurt her foot a little and was kept in her chair, so more than ever fell to Ellen. She wrote:—

"It is as though I had been walking down a long corridor and suddenly had opened a door into the light; when I came in sight of our house to-night and thought of all the people who can be happier because of me, tears of happiness came to my eyes, and I should have been glad if I could have gone down on my knees there and thanked God that I was of use in the world to those whom I love. All the selfish winter of my heart melted and my mind went out to my friend who helped me to find myself and to bring me home again. I suppose this is the road people have to travel to learn the meaning of life. You hear a bird sing by the road and you stop to listen, and by and by your heart starts beating again."

CHAPTER XXVI

When Alec came back in the early summer, he told me he was to stay for the year. The academy had offered him a place in it, and so had another school and he had chosen the academy.

"Isn't the other place better?" I asked him.

He nodded.

"A little better; the experience is as good here."

We did not need to discuss why it was he had stayed. I was a good enough friend of his to be able to ask:—

"Is it fair to Elizabeth?"

"Roberta," he said, "I'm going to give my whole life to Elizabeth as long as it is of use to her, but I have a right to give a year of it partly to Ellen when she needs me." For his insight into Ellen had told him that she needed a hand out to her; during the moments of doubt and moments of return to the dead center in which she had lived so long.

"Seeing Ellen, and seeing her free, won't you care more for her than you ought?" I objected.

"I'll have to get over it if I do. I've thought it out, Roberta. Nothing that I give Ellen takes away from what I give Elizabeth. I care for her just as much as I always did, and I've always cared for Ellen the same."

"Oh, Alec!" I cried, "why does the world have to be so at cross-purposes? Why aren't you free, and why can't you make Ellen care for you? Are you sure that Elizabeth cares for you?"

"It's not for me to think things like that at all, Roberta," he answered. "It would be a poor sort of love I'd bring to Ellen, wouldn't it? I can't take kindness from Elizabeth and wrap myself in the cloak of her sympathy when I need it and throw it away when the sun comes out, even had the unimaginable happened, and Ellen cared for me,—which she won't. Some faiths one has to keep with one's self."

As for Ellen, she accepted Alec's companionship as a matter of course. She had no doubts at all about Alec's devotion to Elizabeth, for Elizabeth was one who compelled sweetness when one spoke of her. She was a little person, appealing and soft, and the sort of woman who attends to the physical wants of the man she loves so kindly that this devotion is almost spiritual. It never occurred to Ellen that she still held any place in Alec's heart or that his early affection for her had been anything more than a boyish devotion he had outgrown for a real love. I think through the autumn and long winter, they both lived in the radiance of their affection for one another; they two were in the light together and the past and future were shut out. Perhaps they were better friends that they were not lovers. They both lived like children in the present, neither one looking into the future, when Alec should no longer be hers, but another woman's.

> "It's good [she wrote] to have something that lasts in one's life. Never for a moment, in all that I've lived through, has my affection faltered for Alec, nor his for me. We have each of us had more absorbing loves than each other, but this steady little flame remains unquenched."

I think in their mutual satisfaction and the consciousness of their own virtue, they did not realize, as high-minded people often do, how this flowering friendship might affect a smaller nature. Elizabeth grew restless under it, and Miss Sarah found out from gossiping people that Elizabeth had not scrupled to do what was little short of spying on Alec.

"I hope," she said to Ellen, "that you're worldly wise enough not to make trouble. Of course, we know that Alec might as well be your brother, but a young woman in love can't be expected to realize it."

Alec was supremely unaware of any discontent on Elizabeth's part; he went over to see her as regularly as he had come home while he was in college, and whatever she felt she kept to herself. I fancy that Alec, whimsical and humorous, large-hearted and kind, would have been hard to approach with a small jealousy. Once in the light of his smile it would have withered up.

It was after more and more of this talk had come to Ellen that I find, for the first time, in her journal a note of emotion about Alec.

"When I hear them tell all the little things she does against you, Alec, my heart weeps, for if she's like that, I must watch you start out on a road of long disillusionment. It's so hard to sit aside and watch sadness and even disgust grow in your eyes, that my heart is heavy, and with unshed tears. What will happen to you whose goodness has come out to meet the goodness in me all your life? Either your own goodness will burn up the you that loves her, or the you that loves her will eat and corrode the you I love. I hope for you the high unhappiness and the sad and hard-gained peace rather than the contented compromise with the little, mean virtues that act as anodynes. Whatever happens to the outward aspect of your life, I wish for you that your spirit may walk free; but oh! I shan't be there to help you in the hard places, I shan't be able to hold out my hand to you as yours has been held out to me."

It was only when she realized that Alec was going out into a life fraught with difficulties for him, since he loved a woman who had it in her power to hurt him so, that Ellen looked at the future, empty of her friend. From this time her journal is full of Elizabeth. From a woman to be taken for granted, some one sweet whom Alec loved, she became a sinister menace. In her little soft person she carried the unhappiness of what had been sweetest in Ellen's life.

CHAPTER XXVII

There came a beautiful spring month where she put the thought of the future from her, for Elizabeth was away on a visit and Ellen could forget her. Alec might have gone to his very wedding-day without Ellen knowing her very own mind and realizing that the dear and long-tested affection had changed its name; and only after he left her would she have wept at the grief of her heart, and, indeed, to me, a close observer, it did not seem to change its complexion at all, and not until the day of Alec's accident was I, a constant third in their party, conscious of any change in them.

You know how disaster fills the air of a little town as a spiritual thunderclap. I remember to this day the sinister feeling I had that something was wrong when I saw two women meet two others in front of my house and stop, talking and gesticulating. I remember the flash that went over me was, "I wonder what's happened"; and then a patter of bare feet and a little flying figure of a lad dashed past, and they would have stopped him, but he made a wild circle around them, crying as he went:—

"Alec Yorke's dead!"

Then I went out and became one of the gesticulating women. Then came the doctor driving from the school; he was waylaid up the street, and we scurried along, young and old, to hear what had happened. It seemed there had been some sort of a boy's prank with some gunpowder, and Alec, pulling away a boy, had been hurt. No, he wasn't dead, but there was a question of his eyesight; one couldn't tell how badly injured he was until the next day. That was all there was to tell. He was resting quietly. Then there was the rattle of wheels, and I saw Ellen driving down the street. She came straight toward us, but she was so drowned in the dolorous contemplation of what had happened that I am sure she did not see us, though at the sight of her face we all turned silent and stared at her; and the doctor dropped an illuminating word:—

"She's going to get Alec's young lady. Coming to he was

rambling on about her, and"—he hesitated—"if the worst should happen it would be a comfort to have her there."

But I, who knew Ellen so well, knew at the sight of her face what it was that had happened to her, and an impulse so deep in me that the words sprang to my lips involuntarily made me cry out, "Ellen, stop. I'm going with you."

She obeyed me mechanically, but she seemed almost unconscious of me as I got in beside her. It was one of those days in spring when the world seems sodden with tears; when every tree drips all the day long. I remember to this day how I felt as I sat there by Ellen's side, fighting back tears until I was sick, for the hopeless tragic tangle of life had overwhelmed me. I wanted to cry with the oblivion of grief that unhappily one seldom knows this side of childhood. It seemed to me that some hidden well of sorrow had been opened from which the tears must gush forth unquenchable. And yet I must not cry, since Ellen sat there like something turned into stone. It was an irony too cruel to be borne that she should drive over this road to bring this alien Elizabeth to Alec.

I knew, as though she had herself told me so, that all life could give her no such sweetness as the right to comfort Alec in his moment of trial, and that life had never given her anything harder than to go seeking another woman to fill the place that she would have been glad to fill herself. And with the same clearness of vision I knew that it was Ellen for whom Alec had called. At the moment of his disaster the old comfortable myth of friendship had ceased, and then Ellen had known that for her Alec was the very foundation of life, woven into its fabric, and that he had always been there. And this knowledge had come so flooding, so overwhelming that it drowned her and with it came the necessity of seeking a stranger for him.

The interminable wet and weeping road over the mountain swarmed with memories of Alec; with the ghosts of the Alec and ourselves of bygone days. It was up this road that we had walked to meet him through that long and difficult winter, and the really glad spots of life were his home-coming. What did "over the mountain" mean, anyway, but Alec? And yet here we were going upon this errand; nor could I have opened my lips to say a word against it, even though I was innerly certain it was Ellen, and not Elizabeth, Alec wanted, for I was bound down by the fierce and narrow-minded code which decreed that, while a woman might refuse a marriage with a man, a man must go through to the bitter end. I had permitted myself one protest and repented of it. As we go on we will throw away all the false loyalties that have crucified so many of us.

Both Ellen and myself faced this as though it was as inevitable as death itself. I do not know how fully she realized what she was doing; I do not know, but I cannot believe that deep down in her heart she thought that Alec didn't care for her. But she had played the game of friendship with Alec too long and too well to think that he gave her anything else but friendship. So we drove, silent, over our beloved road and down the other side of the mountain into the village street whose elms dripped unceasingly, and up to Elizabeth's white, commonplace little house.

There was an added irony to it all in the way she received us in her parlor. She was the type of girl who preserves under all circumstances the little punctilios of life. She didn't permit herself the indiscretion of one surprised look at the sight of our strained faces and our arrival in the midst of a slow-falling, implacable spring rain. It was impossible not to avoid the polite overtures of an ordinary call. If we had come on an important errand it was plain that we should have to make the opening for the telling of that errand ourselves. She was very polite to us, but her politeness hid a mild resentment, for we had represented in life all of Alec that she had never been able to possess; while to us Elizabeth, so pretty in her commonplace way, so decorous, represented the menace of Alec's happiness.

For a moment we bandied polite phrases, or rather Elizabeth and I did, while Ellen sat inert and aloof as she had on the drive over, until all of a sudden she seemed to awaken in a gush of pity for Alec and for Elizabeth. She swept all the little politenesses out of the way with one gesture.

"Elizabeth," said she, "you must put on your things and come with us. Alec's been hurt. His eyesight is perhaps in danger."

There was something deeply sweet in the way she spoke and deeply sweet in the look she gave Elizabeth, and at her complete sincerity and goodness Elizabeth also dropped the politenesses that she was using as a shield against us. The tears that were so easy for her started to her eyes.

"Oh, Ellen!" she cried; "oh, poor Alec!"

"We'd better go, I think, Elizabeth," said Ellen gently.

"I can't go," Elizabeth answered; "I can't go with you, Ellen."

And to the amazed question of our looks: "I can't go because I care for some one else," she told us. "I'd have written to him before," she went on, "but I thought I'd let him wait. He'd let me wait long enough." There was neither spite nor bitterness in her tone as she said this. I think the very best of her came forward to meet us in this moment. At the root of her narrow little nature was a certain childlike candor. "I cared for him too long without having him ever care. I tried to be real patient, but I got tired after a while, Ellen, and it seems good to me to have the whole heart of a man." And then a light whiff of anger flamed up in her. "Why did you come for me anyhow, Ellen Payne," she cried, "when he might need you? You knew all the time it was you he cared for; you knew all the time it was you he wants! Now hurry, hurry back."

The conventionalities had fallen from her, and for the first and last time we saw the Elizabeth for whom Alec had cared.

With this godspeed we started on our long drive back, I full of disquieting fears, full of anguish concerning Alec; Ellen still and withdrawn. After a while the strain of silence told on me and the words forced themselves from my lips: "Oh, I can't bear to think of its happening. I can't bear to think of having his life hurt this way."

As if recalled from a very far distance, Ellen turned her head to me.

"It can't happen, Roberta," said she slowly.

I looked at her curiously. There was just enough light for me to see the outline of her face, and I felt as if she had pulled herself back by some great effort to answer me and that her spirit had been somewhere with Alec, free for the first time. And I felt for the rest of the ride as if in some obscure way he were near us; that Ellen could call to him through the dark.

His mother opened the door for us.

"I'm glad you've come," she said with her profound simplicity. "He's wanted you all his life, Ellen Payne."

So we three women sat ourselves down for the night watch to learn what the morning would bring. Alec's mother sat there, her hands folded, solid as a rock, impassive as fate. She had borne a great deal in her life and had grown strong with it, and whatever happened she would be there to help him. All through my life I shall remember Ellen's face as it was through that long night, for it was the face of one who defies death and disaster; and what I mean only those who have brooded guardingly over the lives of those whom they love will understand. For there comes a moment in the lives of most women and some men when they seem to put their spirits, a tangible thing, between death and disaster and the beloved.

And one more thing I shall remember forever was Alec's voice, as he cried out in his sleep, "Ellen," and again, "Ellen," as though, sunk fathoms deep in pain, he still called for her and his unconscious body groped for her in the darkness. So we sat and waited through the night, until the blessed word came to us at last that all was well with him.

There was only one more entry in the journal and then blank leaves, for I suppose she began another book that belonged to herself and Alec alone. It told of the accident and went on:—

"I felt as if I had been waiting for this one moment all my life; as if all I had ever been and could hope to be concentrated itself in those long hours; as though the arms of my spirit folded themselves around him as I prayed, and as I prayed I knew that my prayer had been answered. I was as certain that it was well with him as if I could penetrate into the future. And that night I knew the meaning of my long life, and that I had only been learning to love enough, so that when he called to me, 'Ellen, Ellen,' I should have learned how to love and how to give."

THE END